The Case of the Missing Raccoon

Disappointed, Amber went to her room. She needed a comforting hug from R.C. But R.C. wasn't in his usual place on her pillow. Then Amber remembered she had left her stuffed raccoon outside on the patio.

The patio swing was empty.

Amber looked under the swing and behind the pots of petunias. She looked under the chairs and table, and in the bushes nearby.

She went back inside and started searching the house. Maybe she had brought R.C. in and forgotten where she had put him. But she couldn't find the raccoon anywhere.

R.C., her most prized possession in the world, was gone.

Tales From Third Grade

Third Grade
Detectives

Candice F. Ransom

Troll Associates

Third Grade
Detectives

It was the last day of school in Mrs. Sharp's third grade class.

Room Six looked somewhat bare. No posters hung on the walls. No drawings or "A" papers were tacked to the bulletin board. But Mrs. Sharp had brought in juice and cookies. The students laughed and talked as they cleaned out their desks.

A cookie and a cup of juice sat on one corner of Amber Cantrell's desk, but she couldn't eat. Her stomach felt fizzy with end-of-the-year excitement.

Amber busily sorted papers, putting her very best schoolwork into a special folder.

Mrs. Sharp had given each student a double-pocket folder for take-home work. Most of the students had decorated their folders with stickers.

Not Amber. Amber Cantrell had to be different.

She had drawn a picture of her stuffed animal, a raccoon named R.C., on the cover of her take-home folder. The raccoon was holding a folder just like Amber's. On the cover of the raccoon's folder was a *smaller* stuffed raccoon holding an even *smaller* take-home folder.

Mrs. Sharp came by to see how she was doing. "Amber, that is the cleverest folder. I just can't get over it."

"Thank you, Mrs. Sharp." Amber sorted swiftly through a stack of arithmetic papers. Math was her worst subject; there wouldn't be any worth taking home.

"How is R.C. these days?" the teacher inquired. Amber had shared her stuffed raccoon with the class several times that year.

"He's fine," Amber answered. "He sits on my pillow a lot these days. I think he's getting lazy."

Mrs. Sharp laughed. "That's very funny! A stuffed animal getting lazy."

"Well, he is." No one knew her stuffed raccoon better than she did.

Her father had given her the raccoon the summer she had turned six. Amber had promptly named him R.C. He was just right for hugging and telling secrets to. R.C. became Amber's constant companion, especially when her father moved out later that same summer.

Now Mrs. Sharp paused at Mindy Alexander's desk, right across the aisle from Amber's.

"How are you doing, Mindy?" she asked.

Mindy frowned over a messy pile of papers. "I don't have any good papers to take home. My mom won't have time to look at this stuff anyway. She's too busy with my little sister. Now that Sarah's crawling, she's into everything."

Mrs. Sharp reached into the pile and pulled out several papers. "Here are some 'A' papers. Of course your mother will want to see these."

"Don't forget your folktale," Amber put in. "Yours was really good."

"Not as good as yours," Mindy said. "Amber's was the best in the class, wasn't it, Mrs. Sharp?"

"Everyone wrote interesting folktales," the teacher replied, moving on. "I enjoyed reading them all."

Secretly, Amber suspected Mrs. Sharp enjoyed reading hers the most. Amber had written about herself, the Third Grade Legend. She *was* a legend in Virginia Run Elementary. Who else had accomplished as much in one year?

"We did lots of neat things this year," Amber said to Mindy. "The neighborhood project . . . the canned book reports—"

"They don't fit in our folder." Mindy placed her tomato juice can covered with the book report "label" on top of the pile.

"No, but don't forget to take it home anyway."

"Okay." Mindy usually agreed with Amber. They were best-best friends.

The summer Amber's father had moved out, Mindy's family moved into the house across the street. Amber and Mindy became friends immediately. Later that fall, they went to first grade at Virginia Run Elementary.

"Hey, Mindy, look at this." Amber held up a paper.

The paper, written in shaky cursive, read *Amber Gillian Cantrell*. At the bottom was a whole row of *o*'s.

Amber remembered the day she was finally able to write her name in cursive. Learning to make smooth, oval-shaped *o*'s was a big achievement, too.

"I'm going to keep this," she said, placing the cursive paper in her take-home folder.

"Uh-oh," Mindy warned. "Here comes trouble."

Amber glanced at the two boys heading their way.

"I hope they don't start talking about their stupid snake club again," she said.

David Jackson and Henry Hoffstedder had started a club to catch and study reptiles. David even had a pet garter snake named Titus.

Amber liked David, even if he did have a pet snake. On Valentine's Day, David had given her a special Valentine. She'd been so thrilled when he proposed to her. Amber was the first girl in third grade to be engaged!

But when David also gave an engagement ring to Delight Wakefield, Amber was not so thrilled. She and Delight had tried to trap David into marrying them both at the same time. The wedding-that-never-happened was a famous event of the past school year. David had learned not to mess around with Amber Gillian Cantrell.

But Amber had forgiven him for two-timing her. "Did you finish your take-home folder?" she asked him.

"Yeah. Didn't take long."

Henry Hoffstedder snickered. "He only has two papers!"

Amber didn't like Henry very much. He was forever teasing the girls. "That's probably two more than you had to put in yours," she replied.

"Is that so?" He pulled a crumpled spelling test from his pocket.

"A 'D minus,'" Amber said scornfully. "You can't even spell 'food.' It has two *o*'s, not one."

"Well, you can have it for a souvenir." Henry crammed the paper in Amber's folder.

"Think you'll pass?" David asked her.

"Of course," she replied airily. "I'm not worried. But *you* should be, Henry."

"Teacher wouldn't dare leave me back," Henry said, as he and David left to get more juice.

Suddenly Amber began to worry.

Would she pass? She hadn't made any failing grades on her report card, but there was always the possibility of being left back. She knew a boy who had repeated second grade because his parents didn't think he was ready for third grade. Suppose Mrs. Sharp didn't think Amber was ready for fourth grade?

"Mindy," she said. "Do you think we'll pass?"

"Sure. Why shouldn't we?" Mindy packed her crayons neatly into the box.

"I don't know," Amber said. "Maybe Mrs. Sharp will leave somebody back so she won't have a whole class of brand-new students next year. Maybe she'll pick me to leave back."

"Remember when you *wanted* to be left back?" Mindy said. "Remember the day you went back to Ms. Lovejoy's class?"

"That was different." Amber squirmed with embarrassment. She didn't want to remember the day she quit third grade and went back to her old second grade class.

Amber had started third grade with high hopes. She believed she had the prettiest name. Her hair was nearly long enough to sit on. That should have made her the most popular kid.

But then a new girl had joined the class. Her

name was Delight Wakefield. Her hair was longer and her name was prettier, too. Delight even had a more interesting stuffed animal, a dog named Row-bear that had come all the way from Paris, France.

Delight quickly became the most popular kid in Room Six. Amber decided she'd had enough of third grade and retreated to the comfort of second grade. But she discovered she wasn't happy there either, so she returned to Mrs. Sharp's class.

Just then Delight came up to Amber's desk.

"You guys are coming over to my house tonight, right?" she asked them both. "Don't forget my end-of-the-year party."

"I'll be there," Mindy replied.

"Me, too," said Amber.

She looked up at Delight. Delight wore her honey-colored hair very short, falling in points over her ears.

Once, Amber had been so jealous of Delight, she grabbed a pair of scissors and cut off a big hunk of Delight's hair. Though it hadn't been easy, Amber had stopped being jealous of Delight. Now Delight was Amber's second-best friend.

"What are we going to do tomorrow?" Delight asked Amber. "It's the first day of summer vacation."

"I know what we're doing the second day of vacation," said Mindy. "Soccer tryouts."

Amber made a face.

"You promised," Mindy reminded her.

"I don't like soccer," Amber said. "But I'll go with you and Delight."

"It'll be fun," Delight said.

Amber didn't think do. She'd rather stay home and read a new Billie Bradley mystery than run around a hot soccer field. Maybe she'd be made captain of the team. She'd like soccer a lot better if she were captain.

Just then Mrs. Sharp went to the front of the class. In her arms was a stack of familiar brown envelopes. Report cards.

"Uh-oh," said Delight. She scurried back to her desk.

Everyone waited nervously. It was time to see who had passed and who had failed.

Mrs. Sharp walked up and down the aisles, passing out report cards.

When the teacher dropped a brown envelope on Amber's desk, Amber's heart stopped for a second. Then she picked up the envelope and opened it. Her eyes skimmed the grades—"A" in Reading, "B" in Spelling, "C" in Math—to the single line at the bottom that said, *Promoted to Fourth Grade.*

"Yes!" Amber cried with relief.

Mindy shrieked with happiness as she opened her own report card. Across the room, Delight gave Amber a thumb's-up. She had passed, too.

David Jackson and Henry Hoffstedder whooped and pounded their desks.

"I can't believe Henry passed," Mindy remarked.

"Mrs. Sharp probably couldn't stand him another year," Amber said.

"I hope Henry's not in our class next year."

Amber was looking over the remarks her teacher had written on the back of her report card.

She leaned toward Mindy. "What does this mean? 'Amber sometimes needs to curb her impulses.' What are impulses?"

"I don't know. Why don't you ask Mrs. Sharp?"

The teacher flicked the lights off and on to get everyone's attention.

"We have just a few minutes before the bell," she reminded them. "Next fall, as fourth-graders, you will be expected to write an essay. It will be called 'How I Spent My Summer Vacation.' "

The class groaned.

"I'm telling you this now so you can be thinking about it this summer," the teacher added.

Amber's fizzy end-of-the-year feeling suddenly went flat, like a glass of stale ginger ale. Who wanted to think about schoolwork during summer vacation?

"We're going to visit my grandmother this summer," Mindy said as she packed her folder and supplies into her knapsack. "Delight's going to Disney World. Where are you going, Amber?"

"Nowhere."

This wasn't exactly true. She was going with her brother and her mother to Pennsylvania to buy quilts for her mother's quilt shop. Still, a trip to Pennsylvania wasn't like going to Disney World.

As Amber loaded her knapsack, she decided she would have to *plan* an exciting summer, instead of letting it just happen. Then she would have something to write about next year in fourth grade.

The bell rang, the last bell of the year.

"Have a great summer, everyone!" Mrs. Sharp said.

The third-graders leaped up with shouts of joy and ran from the classroom, eager to begin their vacation.

Amber paused at Mrs. Sharp's desk, while Mindy and Delight waited in the hall.

"Good-bye, Mrs. Sharp. I hope you have a nice summer."

"You, too, Amber," her teacher replied. "I've enjoyed having you in my class."

"I learned a lot in your room this year. Cursive . . . how to grow seeds . . . even fractions."

"You learned a lot more than cursive and fractions," Mrs. Sharp said.

"Really? What else?"

Her teacher gave her a mysterious smile. "You'll discover all the things you learned, by and by. Now, scoot. Your friends are waiting."

Amber headed for the door, then turned suddenly and walked back to her desk.

"I just want to sit in it one last time," she explained, sliding into the desk that had been her home the entire third grade.

Mindy signaled from the doorway. "Amber, we'll miss the bus!"

As Amber got up, she felt something tug her hair. She had been sitting on her hair! It was finally long enough to sit on!

She skipped out of the classroom. She had forgotten to ask her teacher about that remark on her report card, the part about needing to curb her impulses.

Amber didn't know what impulses were, but she thought a curb had something to do with horses. She pictured a wild runaway horse being reined in.

That was it. Her teacher thought she was like a wild horse.

Wild-horse Amber ran down the hall, giddy with freedom. Her hair streamed out behind her like a mane.

Third grade was over.
Summer vacation was here!

TWO

Amber was awakened the next morning by the shrill cries of birds outside her window. The bus, she thought. I can't be late for school.

Then she remembered it was the first day of summer vacation. She didn't have to catch the bus. She didn't have to go to school. She didn't even have to get out of bed.

She took a library book off her nightstand. It was called *The Clue in the Old Oak Tree*. Settling back with her stuffed raccoon, Amber opened the book.

Since she'd discovered Billie Bradley mysteries, Amber couldn't get enough of them. Billie Bradley was a girl detective who solved all sorts of mysteries. Whenever the police were baffled over a crime, they called in Billie Bradley. Amber wanted to be just like her.

The first day of summer vacation and a new Billie Bradley mystery . . . life was perfect. Sighing happily, Amber started to read.

But the June morning beckoned. She got up, kicking her take-home folder under her bed. She was through with school! She put on shorts and a T-shirt, then padded barefoot out to the kitchen.

Her older brother, Justin, was still asleep. At almost-fourteen, Justin was allowed to stay up later. But her mother should be up, doing chores before she left for work.

The kitchen was empty. Hearing water splashing, Amber followed the sound out the back door.

Her mother was watering the pots of petunias and begonias that lined the patio.

"Hi, Mom," Amber said.

"Morning, sweetie," her mother greeted her. "I'll fix your breakfast in a minute. I need to water my plants first."

Amber sat on the wooden swing. She was in no hurry to eat. She swung back and forth, dangling her feet.

Blue jays and sparrows squabbled at the bird feeder. A bee buzzed around a pot of pink geraniums. Sunlight striking the arching water made a sparkly rainbow. The whole morning seemed to sparkle.

Summer vacation. The two best words in the world.

She could do anything this summer. The possibilities stretched before her like the endless days on the calendar. She could build a fort, dig up buried treasure, climb the highest trees in the woods by the creek. . . .

"Okay, squirt, listen up." Justin slouched before her, wearing his favorite baseball cap backward. "Get me some juice."

"I'll do no such thing," Amber said.

"Mom's left me in charge this summer. You have to do what I say. And I say, get me a glass of juice." He pushed his cap back further to emphasize his authority.

Amber leaped off the swing. Her mother was putting the hose away.

"Mom! Do I have to listen to Justin?"

Mrs. Cantrell kicked off her muddy "garden" shoes. "Amber, we talked about this last night. Justin will be in charge this summer while I'm at work."

"But he's my *brother*," she protested. "He's not old enough to be in charge."

"Justin will be fourteen in a few weeks. He will be going to high school next year. He's old enough and responsible enough to watch you," her mother said.

Old, responsible Justin stuck his tongue out at Amber.

"I don't need a sitter!" Amber cried. "I can watch myself!"

"You've grown up a lot this year," her mother admitted. "But you can't run around without supervision. It won't be only Justin watching you—Mindy's mom will keep an eye on you, too."

Last summer Amber had stayed at Mindy's house during the day while Mrs. Cantrell ran her shop. They had a lot of fun making toys and clothes and books for R.C. and Pearl, Mindy's stuffed penguin. Amber didn't see why she couldn't go over to Mindy's house again this summer.

But Mindy's mother had a baby to take care of. So Mrs. Cantrell had made the decision that Justin would watch Amber. And get paid for doing it! All because he was the older one.

Amber wished *she* was almost-fourteen so she could boss him around. But she wouldn't even be nine until August.

"Justin said I have to listen to him. He said I have to get him a glass of juice," Amber complained to her mother.

"You do have to listen to your brother," Mrs. Cantrell said. "You do *not* have to wait on him. Justin, Amber is not your slave. I don't want to come home every day and hear a long list of gripes either. I expect you two to get along. Remember, this family is a team."

Amber had heard the "team" speech many times since her parents had divorced. It wasn't always easy, with just the three of them.

Two years ago, Amber's father had moved into an apartment in Maryland, over the Potomac River. Amber and Justin usually visited their father on weekends and holidays. This past year, though, Mr. Cantrell had canceled several weekends because he'd visited a lady friend in Philadelphia. Then Amber's father started seeing another lady from his office. Now he wasn't dating anyone and the regular weekend visits had resumed.

Secretly, Amber hoped her father would move out of his apartment and come live with them again. The house on Carriage Street sometimes seemed empty without him.

"Can I count on you two not to fight today?" asked Mrs. Cantrell.

"I guess," Amber said grudgingly. She was still stinging from the realization that Justin was her summer baby sitter.

"Yeah, sure," Justin said.

Mrs. Cantrell smiled. "Good. It's almost time for me to leave. What would you guys like for breakfast?"

"Waffles," Amber replied immediately.

"Pancakes," Justin said at the same time.

Amber stuck her tongue out at Justin. In return, he made an awful face at her.

Mrs. Cantrell sighed. "It's going to be a *long* summer."

Amber ran as fast as she could across her front lawn. The wind blew the streamers of the willow tree east. Amber pumped her legs furiously, trying to beat the wind.

Wild horses were very fast. They could run faster than the wind.

The trouble was, she couldn't *see* the wind. It was hard to race an invisible opponent. Still, her teacher had thought Amber was like a wild horse.

Amber had forgotten to ask her mother about the remarks on her report card. Her mother had come home from work late yesterday and congratulated both Amber and Justin on passing to the next grade. Then they left for Delight's party.

Wild-horse Amber neighed and pawed the air like a rearing stallion.

"What are you doing?" Mindy stood on the sidewalk, holding her little sister's hand.

"I'm a wild horse," Amber replied matter-of-factly. "Want to play? You can be a wild horse, too."

"I have to watch Karen while Mom's putting Sarah down for her nap," Mindy said. Karen was five.

Mindy often had to watch her.

"Can I be a wild horse with you guys?" Karen asked Amber.

Amber tugged Karen's ponytail. "You could be a wild pony."

"Let's wait till Delight gets here," Mindy said. "Maybe by then, the baby will be asleep and Mom will take Karen back home."

"I don't want to go back home!" Karen said, on the verge of pouting. "I want to play wild horses."

"Karen, don't be a pest," Mindy said. To Amber, she added, "Ever since her birthday last month, she's been impossible."

Amber liked Mindy's sister. She thought she was cute.

"We're not playing anything right now," Amber told Karen, sitting cross-legged on the sidewalk. "We're waiting for Delight, okay?"

Delight Wakefield lived up Carriage Street, across Little Rocky Run, where the houses were bigger and newer. Delight didn't have a little sister to watch or an older brother to boss her around. She was an only child. Amber often wished she was an only child.

Delight got to do almost anything she wanted. And she didn't have to share with anyone. The only problem Amber could see with being an only child was that Delight's parents fussed over her a lot.

Mrs. Wakefield was forever making Delight take a bath or eat all of her breakfast before Delight could go out to play. Delight's mother was part-owner of Mrs. Cantrell's quilt shop. At the party last night, Mrs. Wakefield mentioned that she had hired an older woman to stay with Delight while she was at work.

"Wasn't that a neat party last night?" Mindy said.

"*Seven* different kinds of pizza!" Amber commented. "Mr. Wakefield must have ordered every kind there was."

"I was going to have a piece of each, but I got too full." Mindy stretched her legs in front of her and yawned.

"Can I go to the creek?" Karen asked.

"You know you're not allowed to cross the street by yourself," Mindy said.

Karen found a stick and twirled it idly in the dirt. Except for the drone of a distant lawn mower, the neighborhood was silent.

Amber yawned, too. She didn't feel like a wild horse anymore. It was a lazy kind of a day. A day to do nothing.

She suddenly imagined the summer dribbling away in a series of do-nothing days. Time would be wasted waiting for Delight to join them, baby-sitting little sisters, checking in with parents or bossy older brothers.

Billie Bradley never sat idly on the curb. She

had more important things to do, like running her detective agency. Billie Bradley was busy every minute tracking down criminals and solving mysteries. Her life was exciting.

Then Amber remembered the essay Mrs. Sharp had mentioned on the last day of school. All fourth-graders had to write a paper about how they had spent their summer vacation. Amber pictured her paper—a blank page.

What would she have to write about? How she sat on the sidewalk? Billie Bradley did so many things, there were nineteen books about her.

If Amber was going to have an exciting summer, maybe she'd better start making plans now.

"Mindy," she announced. "We have to get organized."

Mindy smothered another yawn. "What for?"

"We have to do something special. We can't just waste our entire summer doing nothing."

"I like doing nothing," Mindy said. "Anyway, tomorrow we have soccer tryouts. That's something."

"But that's tomorrow," Amber said. "We need to get cracking today."

"It's not even ten o'clock," Mindy protested. "And it's our vacation. Why do we always have to be doing stuff?"

Across the street, Mrs. Alexander appeared in her front door and waved. That was her signal to Mindy that Sarah was finally asleep.

"Okay, Karen," Mindy said. "Mom's not busy. Go home."

"I don't want to go home," Karen whined. "I want to play with you and Amber."

"We'll play another time," Amber said. "Right now your mother wants you."

Karen sulkily crossed the street and went into her house.

Just then Delight hurried down from the corner.

"I came as fast as I could," she said, sitting down with them. "My mom made me eat oatmeal."

Amber looked at her with sympathy. Oatmeal on a cold day was bad enough, but in the summer? Yuck!

"That was a great party last night," Mindy said to Delight.

"Yeah," Amber agreed. "It was fun."

"Glad you had a nice time," Delight said, somewhat glumly. She placed her elbows on her knees and propped her chin in her hands. She didn't seem very happy, considering this was the first day of summer vacation.

Amber figured Delight was bored already. She would take care of that.

"We're getting organized," Amber told her. "We can't sit around and waste the whole summer. We have to do something."

"You keep talking about doing something," Mindy said. "Do you have any ideas?"

Amber had been thinking for the past several minutes. She had a terrific idea. Probably the best idea she had ever thought up. The others would jump with excitement when they heard her terrific new idea.

Now she said, "You know those Billie Bradley books I've been reading?"

Mindy groaned. "Are you kidding? That's all you talk about!"

"Well, you know Billie Bradley has her own detective agency. We could do that."

Delight seemed only mildly interested. "A detective agency?"

"I even thought of a name," Amber went on. "The Carriage Street Crime-Busters."

It was an impressive name. If anything, the name alone should hook them.

"The Carriage Street Crime-Busters," Mindy repeated. "We do live on Carriage Street."

"And we can bust crimes!" Amber said. "We'll all be detectives, just like in the Billie Bradley books. We'll take cases and solve them and make a lot of money. Of course, I'll be the head detective."

"Why you?" asked Delight. "How come you get to be the head detective?"

"Because I'm the one who reads the Billie

Bradley books," Amber stated. "And it's my idea. Don't you want to be a detective?"

"I don't know," Delight said without enthusiasm.

"What about you, Mindy?" Amber asked.

Mindy just shrugged.

Amber stood up. She knew the detective agency was a great idea. The others would come around. Mindy always did what Amber did. Delight would, too.

Briskly brushing off her shorts, she said, "Let's go. It's time for the Carriage Street Crime-Busters to get to work."

Chapter THREE

The Crime-Busters walked up Carriage Street, looking for a mystery to solve.

"If only someone would rob a bank," Amber said hopefully. "We could catch them and get the reward."

"There isn't a bank around here," Mindy pointed out.

"Well, maybe we can find a box of hidden jewels in an old mansion."

That had happened in book number three of the Billie Bradley series. Amber glanced around, as if expecting a stately old mansion to suddenly spring up among the modest houses that lined the street.

"There aren't any mansions around here either." Mindy was disgustingly practical, as usual.

Amber stopped to scratch a mosquito bite. "Boy, what a dull neighborhood. No banks, no mansions.

How are we ever going to find a crime to solve in this dumb place?"

Delight was watching two distant figures heading toward the creek. "Hey, isn't that David and Henry? I wonder what they're doing?"

Amber shielded her eyes from the sun. "They're acting awfully suspicious. We ought to see what they're up to."

"They don't look like they're up to anything much," Mindy observed.

"Well, I'm the head detective, and I say we follow them!"

"What if I want to be the head detective?" Mindy said.

"Or me?" chimed in Delight.

Amber frowned at them. Why were they being so stubborn all of a sudden?

"The detective agency is *my* idea," she insisted. "So I'm the head detective. Now, follow me."

Bending low, she scuttled along the sidewalk. It was hard to run in this position, but Billie Bradley always followed criminals without being seen. Then Amber tripped and fell.

Mindy helped her up. "Are you okay? Why are you running all bent over like that?"

"So they won't see us. That's the way Billie Bradley trails criminals." Amber rubbed her knee.

"David and Henry are boys, not criminals,"

Mindy said. "Anyway, they can't even see us. They're already in the woods."

"Hurry! We don't want to lose them!"

The Crime-Busters ran down the street until they came to the bridge that crossed Little Rocky Run. Then they turned onto the bike path that twisted along the creek bank. They hid in the bushes off the bike path.

"There they are," Delight whispered.

"I was right," Amber said triumphantly. "They *are* acting strange. I bet they've committed some big crime. Why else would they be sneaking around like that?"

Both boys were stooped over some object the girls could not see.

"They probably stole a famous statue from a museum," Amber guessed. "It's worth thousands and thousands of dollars and they're going to sell it and make a lot of money."

In *The Case of the Screaming Bell,* Billie Bradley had stopped two desperate men from stealing a famous statue. David and Henry certainly looked desperate, the way they were concealing the object.

"They're really acting guilty," Amber said.

Delight shushed her. "I think they heard us!" She ducked lower, but it was too late.

"All right, you girls," David called. "We see you. Come on out."

The Crime-Busters stood up slowly. "Watch out," Amber warned. "They might make a break for it."

But the suspects made no attempt to escape. David crouched over the object, blocking it from their view.

Henry Hoffstedder scowled at Amber. "Why are you spying on us? Don't you goofy girls have anything better to do?"

"What are *you* doing, sneaking through the woods like that?" Amber accused.

"None of your beeswax!"

"David will tell me." Amber smiled at her former boyfriend. "What are you hiding?"

If it was a famous statue, she planned to yank it away from him, run over the bridge to Delight's house, and stay there until it was safe to go to the police.

David glanced up at Henry. "Should I show them?"

Henry grinned wickedly. "Yeah. Go ahead."

"Okay, girls, you asked for it." David opened the door of a small wire cage and whipped out a long black snake.

Amber screamed and leaped back. Delight scurried behind a tree, shrieking at the top of her lungs. Mindy ran back to the bushes.

"Get that thing away from me!" Amber screeched.

David waved the snake over his head, making Mindy and Delight scream even louder.

"Don't you like him?" he said, laughing. "You're hurting his feelings carrying on like that. Come pet his little head."

"Put that horrible thing back in the cage right this minute!" Amber demanded.

David put the snake back into the cage. It coiled around a branch, licking out a forked red tongue. Amber shuddered. She would never understand how boys could touch anything so gross.

Henry was laughing so hard, he fell on the ground. "I wish I had a camera! You should see your face!"

"I'm glad you think it's so funny," Amber said with as much sarcasm as she could manage. Her legs were still shaking. "Is that your big secret? That horrible snake?"

"Yeah," David said, latching the cage door securely. "What did you think we had? A million dollars?"

His guess came so close to the truth, Amber was even angrier. "How come you were sneaking around if you only had a dumb old snake?" She felt cheated out of her first case.

"It's kind of hard to catch snakes if you make a lot of noise," Henry replied. "With all the racket you girls just made, you probably scared off all the snakes in the whole county. Now we'll never find anything else for our club, thanks to you."

Amber blew out a breath of disgust. "That stupid snake club!"

"Reptile club," David corrected. "We are starting a reptile zoo. We're going to catch snakes and lizards and stuff and let people see them."

"For an admission," Henry added.

"I wouldn't pay a cent to see a bunch of snakes," Amber declared.

As she stalked away, David called, "We won't charge you any admission, Amber. But you have to hold one of the snakes!"

"Fat chance!" Amber yelled back.

The boys had tricked her, and made her look like an idiot. This had never happened to Billie Bradley.

The first big case of the Carriage Street Crime-Busters was a dud.

The detective agency stood on the street corner. It was almost time for lunch.

"See you guys later?" Amber asked. Maybe a terrible crime would be committed by then, and they'd have a real case to solve.

But both Mindy and Delight had someplace to go. Promising to meet early the next morning for the soccer tryouts, the members of the detective agency split up and went their separate ways.

Amber went inside her house.

Justin was watching an old war movie on TV. Amber flopped down on the sofa with him. She watched for a few minutes, but quickly became restless.

"Can you turn the channel?" she asked. "See if there are any cartoons on."

"I'm watching this," Justin told her. "When it's over, you can watch what you want."

"What's for lunch?"

"Tuna salad," he replied. "It's in the refrigerator."

"Some baby sitter," she said scornfully. "I have to fix my own lunch."

She went into the kitchen and made a tuna sandwich. She arranged the sandwich, a carton of raspberry yogurt, and a banana on a tray and carried the tray out onto the patio.

Then she went back into the house to get her stuffed raccoon off her pillow and her library book. R.C. and a Billie Bradley mystery made the best company.

It was nice eating outside in dappled sunshine, with the birds singing in the trees. When she had finished her lunch, Amber curled up in the swing next to R.C. and read *The Clue in the Old Oak Tree*. Instantly, she was involved in the story about a missing will.

Billie Bradley had the neatest life. People came to her with mysteries to solve. Her friends didn't argue over who would be head detective. They knew Billie Bradley was the smartest, and she was never wrong. Billie Bradley didn't have any awful boys with snakes getting in her way either.

The book was so thrilling, Amber wasn't aware the afternoon had passed until her mother stood in the doorway.

"Here you are," Mrs. Cantrell said. "Justin said you'd been reading all afternoon."

"Oh, hi, Mom."

"I stopped at the store. Will you help me put the groceries away?"

Amber went into the kitchen. She unpacked bags, noting with pleasure that her mother had bought her favorite cereal this week. She also noticed there was a large package of pork chops. Her father loved pork chops.

"Is Daddy coming over for supper this week?" Amber asked hopefully.

Her father occasionally ate supper at their house. It was like old times, having her father sit in his place at the table. If her father kept coming over, maybe her parents would get back together.

"No," Mrs. Cantrell answered. "Why do you ask?"

"The pork chops," Amber said. "Daddy loves pork chops."

"So does Justin. I bought your favorite cereal and his favorite meat this week."

The phone rang. Amber answered it. It was her father.

"Daddy, we were just talking about you."

"Nothing bad, I hope. Can I speak to your mother, pumpkin?" he asked.

Amber handed the phone over to her mother. Then she went into the living room. They had a rule in their house: Phone conversations were private.

But as Amber sat on the couch, she thought about the book she had just finished. Billie Bradley eavesdropped all the time. That was how she found out the secret will was hidden in the old oak tree.

If Amber eavesdropped on her mother's phone conversation, she might find out whether her parents were getting back together.

Amber crept up to the kitchen doorway, staying just out of sight.

"Uh-huh," Mrs. Cantrell was saying as she put packages of chicken in the freezer. "Well, I don't know."

This wasn't very interesting information. Her mother could have been talking to anyone—Mindy's mother, the plumber.

"We'll discuss it when you pick the kids up this weekend," Mrs. Cantrell said.

Discuss what? Amber wondered. Maybe her

parents were going to talk about getting back together.

The day her father moved back home would be the happiest day of her life. Then she would have two parents, like Mindy and Delight. And they could all go places together, instead of her and Justin going away every weekend to Maryland.

"See you Saturday." Hanging up the receiver, Mrs. Cantrell said loudly, "All right, Amber. I know you're there. Come in here."

Shamefaced, Amber stepped into the kitchen. Billie Bradley never got caught!

"Why were you listening to my conversation?" her mother asked. "You know the rule."

"I wanted to find out if you and Daddy were getting back together," Amber replied.

Her mother sighed. "Amber, I have told you this many times before. Your father and I are not getting back together."

"But he comes over for supper . . . and he calls you!"

"We always have things to discuss concerning you and Justin," her mother explained. "But that's all. Your father and I have separate lives and that is not going to change."

"Not ever?" Amber didn't want to believe what her mother was telling her.

"It's very doubtful."

Disappointed, Amber went into her room. She needed a comforting hug from R.C. But R.C. wasn't in his usual place on her pillow. Then she remembered she had left him outside on the patio.

The patio swing was empty.

Amber looked under the swing and behind the pots of petunias. She looked under the chairs and table, and in the bushes nearby.

She went back inside and started searching the house. Maybe she had brought him in and forgotten where she had put him. But she couldn't find the raccoon anywhere.

She rushed down to the basement where Justin was working out in the "gym" he had set up.

"Have you seen R.C.?" she asked him.

"Don't tell me that dopey stuffed animal is lost." Her brother lifted his homemade barbell, a broomstick with two sand-filled plastic bottles tied on the ends.

"Yes! I can't find him!" Amber's voice rose with panic.

"Did you look in the house?"

Amber nodded.

"Where was he last?"

"Outside on the swing. But he isn't there now!" Amber wailed.

R.C., her most prized possession in the world, was gone.

The Carriage Street Crime-Busters had a crime to solve at last—the case of the missing raccoon.

After supper, Amber called Mindy. "There's been a terrible crime committed," she reported in a low voice, just like Billie Bradley used. "At my house."

"What?" Mindy asked. "What happened?"

"I can't talk about it over the phone," Amber said mysteriously.

"Amber! What *is* it?"

"Tell you tomorrow." Amber hung up, satisfied that Mindy was dying of curiosity. Now she would take the detective agency more seriously.

Then Amber called Delight. For some reason, Delight didn't ask any questions about the crime. She seemed anxious to get off the phone.

"My father just got home," Delight said. "And a big truck just pulled up in our driveway."

Amber was interested in the big truck, but felt her news was more important.

"What time can you come over tomorrow?" Amber asked her.

"I'm not sure," Delight said. "Why don't you guys come to my house?"

"Because," Amber said, "it's my detective agency. Everyone comes to *my* house."

"We have soccer tryouts at nine," Delight reminded her. "Why don't you come to my house early? Then we can talk on the way to the park."

"All right," Amber agreed reluctantly. "Mindy and I will be at your house around eight-thirty. But next time, everybody comes here."

She hung up and went into her room. Her bed looked bare without R.C. perched in his usual spot on her pillow. Who would have stolen a stuffed raccoon? And why?

Emptying an old shoe box, she began filling it with detective equipment: a small notebook and pencil for writing down clues and names of suspects; a plastic compass that pointed south instead of north, but still might come in handy; a magnifying glass for examining fingerprints; and a water bottle, in case they had to track the criminal through wild territory.

From her brother's room, Amber swiped a fake

FBI badge from his desk. Justin had bought the badge on a field trip to Washington, D.C. Her brother would never miss it, and the badge gave Amber a feeling of authority. Billie Bradley wore a medal given to her by the chief of police.

Mrs. Cantrell came in later to tuck Amber in bed.

"I don't know how I'll sleep without R.C.," Amber said, suddenly feeling forlorn. The raccoon had been her constant nighttime companion for the last two years.

"Are you sure you looked everywhere?" Mrs. Cantrell asked. "You could have misplaced him."

Amber shook her head. "Somebody took him. Right off the swing on the patio. That's where I left him. My raccoon was kidnapped."

"Raccoon-napped is more like it."

"It's not funny, Mom."

Her mother leaned over to kiss her forehead. "I know. I'm just trying to make you feel better. Tomorrow when I get home, we'll turn the house upside-down. We'll find R.C."

Her mother left then, leaving the door open a crack. A wand of light from the hallway lay across Amber's bed. She could hear the reassuring sounds of the TV in the living room.

She turned this way and that, trying to get comfortable. Something was missing. She usually fell asleep with R.C. in her arms. During the night, she often shoved the raccoon to one side, but she always went to sleep with the stuffed animal snuggled close.

As she tossed on her pillow, Amber made a vow. If it took her the entire summer, she would find the culprit who stole her most prized possession.

"Okay," Mindy said as soon as Amber answered the door. "What's this terrible crime?"

"I'll tell you when we're at Delight's."

"Amber! You said you'd tell me tomorrow. Well, it's tomorrow. So tell me."

"When we're all together." Amber enjoyed dragging out the mystery. No one had seemed too interested in the detective agency yesterday. Now she had Mindy's complete attention.

"Justin!" she yelled. "I'm leaving!" She closed the front door behind her and tucked the shoe box under her arm.

"What's that?" Mindy asked.

"Detective stuff," said Amber. "I'll show you at Delight's."

"Why won't you tell me now? I'm supposed to be your best-best friend."

"You are," Amber said. "I just don't want to say everything twice."

It felt good being in charge. People would come to her detective agency with lost wills and missing emerald necklaces for her to find. Soon Amber's detective skills would be known all over the world. She'd be as famous as Billie Bradley.

Amber and Mindy walked up Delight's street. Suddenly Mindy pointed. "Hey! Look at all the kids at Delight's. I wonder what's going on?"

A crowd of kids pressed against the fence that divided the Wakefields' front and back yards.

"Something must have happened," Amber said.

She and Mindy broke into a run. Amber reached the front porch first and stabbed the doorbell.

A gray-haired lady came to the door. Amber figured this was Delight's new sitter, but she had no time for introductions.

She brushed past her, calling Delight's name.

"Young lady," the woman said sternly. "Delight is in the backyard. Is she expecting you?"

"Yeah. I'm Amber. And this is Mindy. I was just worried about her," Amber explained.

"She's all right. And she is expecting you, Amber. I'm Mrs. Figley." The woman smiled. "You're an impulsive one, aren't you?"

Amber flushed. "Well, I saw all those kids—"

"Oh, they want to see Delight's new pool," Mrs. Figley said. Amber and Mindy exchanged a glance. New pool?

Just then Delight breezed in through the patio doors. She wore a red swimsuit. Her short hair was sleek and wet, like a seal's.

"Hey, guys!" she greeted. "I should have told you to bring your bathing suits. Amber, remember that truck I told you about on the phone? Wait'll you see what they brought!"

She led the way onto the patio. In the middle of the backyard sat a brand-new pool. Not a babyish plastic wading pool, but a huge swimming pool. It even had a water slide.

"It took the pool men all evening to set it up," Delight said. "Then another truck came and filled it with water."

"Wow!" Mindy exclaimed. "Your very own pool!"

Amber and Mindy both belonged to the neighborhood pool, but they could only go when either Amber's mother or Mindy's mother was free to take them.

Now Delight had a pool of her own. All she had to do was walk out the back door and jump in.

The kids were trying to scale the high board fence. A few hung on the gate. They cast longing glances at the pool.

Delight cupped her hands into a megaphone. "Nobody's allowed in the pool unless you bring a grown-up. My mom's rule. Sorry."

The kids moved away from the fence with groans of dismay and filed out of the yard.

Amber gawked in wonder at the inviting turquoise water. No wonder every kid in the neighborhood wanted to come in.

"Boy, Delight, you're really lucky," she said enviously. "Is this a birthday present or something?"

"No," Delight said. "My birthday isn't till September. My dad gave it to me because—just because," she finished lamely.

Amber was even more envious. Mr. Wakefield had bought Delight a swimming pool just for fun, not because it was her birthday or Christmas.

"I wish my father would buy us a pool," Mindy said. "But I know he can't afford it."

"My mom is having a fit over this pool," Delight told them. "She's scared somebody will fall in and drown. My dad's going to put a new lock on the gate tonight. But you guys can go swimming if it's okay with your moms."

"I'm going back home and get my suit as soon as the tryouts are over," Mindy said eagerly.

"The tryouts!" Delight dashed into her room to change. She came out a few minutes later wearing a T-shirt and shorts. "Let's go or we'll be late."

"What about our meeting? We have a crime to solve!" Amber couldn't believe her friends were more interested in swimming and soccer tryouts than in solving a terrible crime.

"Tell us at the soccer field," Mindy said, running out the door.

Amber and Delight followed, hurrying up the

hill to the park.

Kids milled about on the playing field. Amber spotted several kids from school, including David Jackson and Henry Hoffstedder.

If Amber made the team, she'd be playing soccer Tuesday and Thursday mornings. That would take a lot of her detective time. Billie Bradley sometimes played softball, but never when she had an important case to solve.

"How long will this take?" she asked Mindy.

"It depends," Mindy said, retying her shoelace. "After the tryouts we might have practice. It's up to the coach, I guess."

Amber saw a woman carrying a clipboard and wearing a whistle around her neck. She blew the whistle, and the kids formed a line.

"Come on," Delight urged Amber. "They're starting."

Kicking was first. Amber was a terrible kicker. As she waited nervously for her turn, she wondered why she let Mindy talk her into these stupid tryouts.

Mindy kicked the ball neatly into the goal. Even Delight kicked pretty well.

When it was Amber's turn, she kicked hard at the ball and missed, nearly flying upside-down. Henry laughed from the sidelines.

"You'll get another chance," Mindy told Amber as she took her place at the end of the "do-over" line.

Determined to do better, Amber kicked furiously the second time, guiding the soccer ball into the goal in record time. The kids were yelling, probably envious of her speed and skill.

"You kicked the ball into the opponent's goal," the coach informed her.

Amber failed kicking. She also failed running. She could run like a wild horse when she had plenty of space, but she couldn't run fast dodging kicks and trying to remember the rules.

"It's okay," Mindy reassured her. "That boy over there is even worse."

The coach announced the team captains. Henry Hoffstedder was the captain of one team. Mindy was captain of the other. They both got special blue-and-white T-shirts to wear during games.

Then the coach began naming the team members. She called David Jackson's name, and Delight Wakefield's name. All the kids' names, it seemed, were called. She even called the name of the boy who ran worse than Amber. But she didn't call Amber's name. Amber and one other girl were left unchosen.

Amber couldn't believe it. "I didn't make the team!"

"Maybe somebody will drop out," Delight said. "Then the coach will call you."

"I don't care about the stupid team," Amber said, though she really did. It was embarrassing to be left out.

Mindy put on her blue-and-white shirt. "The coach wants us to practice," she said. "Will you wait for us, Amber?"

"We have a crime to solve and I haven't even told you yet!" Amber cried. "Now you have to play soccer."

"Tell us now, quick," Delight said. "We have a few minutes."

Billie Bradley never had to describe her cases on a soccer field while waiting for a practice to start. People came to *her* and begged her to take their case.

"R.C.'s been stolen," Amber blurted out. "Yesterday I left him on the patio swing when I went inside for a minute. When I came out again, he was gone." She paused to let this shocking news sink in.

"Somebody stole your stuffed raccoon?" said Delight. "Who would take a stuffed animal?"

"A very desperate person," Amber said. "We have to catch him. Or her. Nobody steals my raccoon and gets away with it."

"Are you sure R.C. was stolen?" Mindy asked. "Maybe he fell off the swing. Did you look—"

"I looked everywhere!" Amber cried. "R.C. is not in the house or in the yard! He's gone!"

"Okay, okay," Mindy said. "Don't get excited."

"You'd get excited, too, if somebody stole Pearl."

Pearl was Mindy's stuffed penguin. Mindy said, "Sarah is using my penguin to chew on. Mom says she's teething. The baby, not my penguin."

Delight and Mindy giggled at this.

"Will you guys be serious?" Amber demanded. "A terrible crime has been committed and you make jokes."

The coach blew the whistle again.

"Got to go," Mindy said. "Come on, Delight."

"The trail is getting colder by the minute," Amber wailed. "We have to start looking!"

"We'll help you find R.C.," said Mindy. "After the game."

"Wait for us," Delight said, running after Mindy. "Then we'll get busy on the case."

Amber didn't feel like hanging around a hot, dusty soccer field until her friends were free. She walked home alone, sure of one thing: Billie Bradley would never have failed to make the soccer team.

Chapter FIVE

Amber lifted the huge, fan-shaped leaves of the August lily and peered into the deep green foliage. A spider, annoyed by the intrusion, sidled away to find more privacy.

With a sigh, Amber sat back on her heels. Ever since she'd come back from soccer tryouts, she'd been searching her backyard. She'd looked under every bush, but had been unable to find a single clue. Not even a footprint. Whoever had kidnapped R.C. had been very clever. He or she had stolen her raccoon without leaving a trace. Even Billie Bradley would be stumped.

Just then her brother came out on the patio. "Lunch!" he yelled.

Amber didn't move.

"I'm not calling you twice," her brother said.

"Don't eat, see if I care."

"I'm looking for R.C.," she told him.

"You and that stupid stuffed animal. Haven't you found it yet?"

"No." Suddenly Amber began to cry. "I've looked and looked, Justin. I can't find him anywhere. Why would anybody steal my raccoon?"

"Maybe it was another raccoon. A real one. She liked the looks of R.C. and made off with him." He brushed her chin lightly with his fist. "Come on, squirt. Let's eat, and then I'll help you hunt."

Amber's tears stopped. "Would you really?" Her brother rarely went out of his way to do anything for her.

"I've got nothing better to do."

In the house, they ate turkey sandwiches, with juice pops for dessert.

"How were the tryouts?" Justin asked.

Amber wrinkled her nose. "I didn't make the team."

"You don't like soccer anyway," Justin pointed out.

"No, but—" She swallowed. "I was practically the only kid who didn't make the team. Me and one other girl. Now I'll have to wait for Mindy and Delight on Tuesdays and Thursdays. We won't be able to do anything till the afternoon."

Justin pushed back his chair. "Well, we can do

something now. Let's go look for R.C."

They went out on the patio.

"Now," Justin began. "You have to use a system when you're hunting for something. You know, logic. Where was the victim last seen?"

Amber pointed to the swing. "Right there."

"Okay." Justin strode over to the swing. "Let's say he fell off. What would be the most logical place to look?"

Amber glanced around. "I guess behind those big pots. But I looked there already."

"I'll look again." Justin checked behind the terra-cotta planters. "Not there. The air-conditioning unit is the next closest place."

"I've looked there, too. R.C. didn't fall off the swing and land behind a pot or the air conditioner. Somebody stole him!"

Justin straightened up from looking behind the air-conditioning unit. "Who would steal a ratty old stuffed raccoon?"

"R.C. is not ratty!" Amber said indignantly. "He's famous! I took him to school and to Mom's shop. Everybody knows him. He's my most prized possession."

Her brother sighed. "Amber, has it occurred to you that R.C. might be gone forever?"

Quick tears made her blink. She pictured R.C., with one lopsided ear from where she had pulled on it and the fur on the left side of his face worn off from hugging.

Never see her beloved raccoon again? The possibility was too horrible to consider.

"No," she said emphatically. "I don't believe it. I'll get him back. Even if I have to search all summer."

Mindy and Delight came over as soon as they had eaten lunch.

"Our team won," Mindy reported.

"I'm on Mindy's team," Delight added. "We named ourselves the Blues. Henry's team is called the Pythons—"

Amber cut in briskly. "If you don't mind, we have work to do."

Mindy glanced at Delight, then shrugged. "Sure. That's why we came straight over—to look for R.C."

Amber was prepared for an entire day of detective work. She'd stuck the notebook in the back pocket of her shorts, jammed the magnifying glass in the other pocket, attached the water bottle to a shoulder strap, and pinned on her FBI badge. If she had to question anyone, she wanted to look official.

"You look like you're going on a safari," Delight remarked. "Do we really need all that stuff?"

"You never know where the trail will lead," Amber said, quoting from the last Billie Bradley mystery she had read. "Billie Bradley is always ready for anything, and so am I."

Moving toward the door, Amber nearly toppled over. She was so loaded down, she had trouble keeping her balance.

"Maybe you'd better empty some of that water," Justin suggested. "You're not going to the Sahara, you know."

Ignoring him, Amber led the way out of the house, swinging her arms to match her purposeful stride.

Mindy and Delight hustled after her.

"What are we doing?" Delight wanted to know.

"We're going to find R.C. The Carriage Street Crime-Busters are conducting a house-to-house search." Amber had learned about that technique in *The Case of the Stolen Necklace.*

Mindy's tone was skeptical. "You mean, knock on every door in the neighborhood and ask if they've seen a stuffed raccoon?"

The plan sounded ridiculous even to Amber, but it was the only idea she had at the moment.

As they passed the houses on their block, Delight asked, "Aren't we supposed to be knocking on doors?"

"We'll start at the other end of the neighborhood."

At the end of Carriage Street, Amber turned down Buggy Whip Lane. She headed for the third house on the left.

"You skipped the first two houses," Mindy pointed out.

"We'll get them on our way back." Actually, Amber was nervous about knocking on strange people's doors to ask if they'd seen a stuffed raccoon. She decided to begin with familiar territory.

"This is David Jackson's house," Mindy observed.

"I know." Amber climbed the porch steps and rang the doorbell.

David answered the door. His eyebrows rose when he saw Amber, Mindy, and Delight standing on his porch.

"Hi, guys. Hey, Mindy, that was some game you played this morning. But the Pythons will beat you next week."

"Fat chance," Mindy said.

Amber cleared her throat loudly. They were not here to talk about soccer!

"We're here on official business," she stated, tapping her FBI badge. "We're investigating the kidnapping of my stuffed raccoon."

Just then Henry Hoffstedder popped his head around the door. "A kidnapped stuffed animal?" he jeered. "Amber Cantrell, you get crazier every day."

"And you get dumber every day, Henry Hoffstedder," Amber shot back. "If you don't mind, I was talking to David. Have you seen R.C.?" she asked him.

David shook his head. "I haven't seen R.C. since the last time you brought him to school. You think somebody stole him?"

As he was talking, Amber looked past him into the hallway. Sitting beside a table was a cloth-covered shape. The shape matched the shape of R.C.

Amber drew in her breath. A clue! But how could she get in there to see what it was? Billie Bradley never waited to be asked in. Billie simply crawled through windows or stormed through front doors to catch her criminals.

"Excuse me," Amber said, barging by the boys. "I see something suspicious." She ran over to the mysterious shape and grabbed the cloth cover.

"No, don't!" David cried.

Amber snatched off the cover. And screamed.

Underneath was a small bird cage. But there was no bird in the cage. A slick, blue-striped lizard scrambled for safety behind a rock.

Henry laughed.

Amber quickly threw the cover over the cage. "Why didn't you tell me you had some awful lizard in there!"

"I tried to warn you." David replaced the cover neatly, making comforting noises to the lizard. "And he's a skink. He's the newest member of our reptile zoo."

"Reptile zoo?"

"Yeah," David said. "We've got a bunch of reptiles in cages out back. Want to see? We'll let you girls look for free."

"No, thanks." Amber shuddered.

"You scared Punky," Henry accused.

"He scared me first," Amber said. "And what kind of a name is that for a lizard?"

"It's a good name." Henry picked up the cage. "What did you think this was anyway?"

"I thought it might be R.C."

David seemed shocked. "You don't really believe I'd steal R.C., do you? I mean, R.C.'s like a member of your family."

"I have to follow every lead," Amber told him. "I can't imagine what happened to him. One minute he was on the swing in my yard, the next minute he was gone."

"I hope you find him," David said.

"Me, too." Amber went back outside where Mindy and Delight were waiting. "We're conducting a house-to-house search for R.C."

Henry followed her out with Punky's cage. "Now the whole neighborhood will know how crazy you are, Amber Cantrell."

"Be quiet, Henry," Amber said. She was in no mood for him or skinks today.

"You know what you ought to do?" David suggested to Amber.

"What?"

"Put up fliers. You know, like people do when they lose their dog or cat."

"R.C. isn't lost," Amber said. "He's stolen."

"But at least people would be on the lookout for him."

Mindy nudged Amber. "That's a great idea. We could put posters all over the neighborhood. Then we won't have to knock on doors. A lot of people aren't home anyway. They're at work."

"Good point," Amber agreed. "Okay, we'll make up a bunch of fliers."

"If you bring some over, I'll put them up around here," David offered.

"Thanks," Amber said, pleased her former boyfriend cared about her missing raccoon.

As they came to Delight's house, Delight said, "I know what we can do. We'll make the posters at my place. I've got tons of posterboard left over from school. Then we can swim before we put them up."

Mindy was all for the idea. "Great! Amber, let's go ask my mom. You can call yours."

Delight unlocked the gate and they went into the backyard. The pool glittered invitingly in the sun. It would be so easy to forget about the search and just spend a lazy day at Delight's.

Remembering her vow to find R.C. no matter what, Amber said, "I can work better at my house.

Come on, you guys. The Crime-Busters have a lot of work to do."

Mindy scuffed her tennis shoe. "Gee, Amber, I'd rather stay at Delight's. Why can't we make the posters here?"

"I just told you, I work better at my house." She blew out an angry breath. "You can't stay either. You have to go home and ask your mother anyway."

"I can call her. If I go home, Karen will want to come, too. She loves to go swimming." Mindy glanced longingly at the pool. "It's so hot today—"

"Mindy! You said you'd help me!"

"I am," Mindy said. "And so is Delight. If we make the fliers here. I don't want to spend the whole day working."

"You haven't worked all day. You played soccer all morning," Amber reminded her.

"That's work," Mindy said. "It was a tough game."

"I don't care about the stupid game! I want to find R.C.!"

"We will, Amber," said Delight. "After we go swimming. Even Billie Bradley takes a break now and then, doesn't she?"

Mindy giggled.

Amber felt her chest swell with fury. How dare they make fun of the greatest girl detective in the history of the world?

"I'm going to make fliers," she said angrily. "You guys can goof off all you want." Turning on one heel, she left the Wakefields' yard.

"Let her go," she heard Mindy say to Delight. "When Amber gets like this, you can't talk to her."

Mindy was a traitor. She didn't care a bit about Amber's mission. She only pretended to be concerned about R.C. All she really cared about was having fun.

Amber couldn't understand why her best-best friend was behaving this way.

Then, with a jolt, she remembered something she had read in *The Clue in the Old Oak Tree*. "Everyone is a suspect," Billie Bradley had said. "Trust no one."

She certainly couldn't trust Mindy, not the way she had acted today.

Could Mindy be the raccoon-napper? Was *she* the one who had stolen R.C.?

Mindy Alexander, Amber decided firmly, was suspect Number One.

Chapter SIX

When she got home, Amber took out her notebook. On her suspect list she wrote, *Number One. Mindy.*

Why would her best-best friend steal her most prized possession? Mindy had never seemed jealous of Amber's stuffed animal. But R.C. was a lot nicer than Pearl, Mindy's stuffed penguin.

She couldn't figure out Mindy's motive, so she dragged sheets of posterboard from her closet. After lining up her markers, she began lettering the first flier.

Lost. Stuffed raccoon named R.C. Has a striped tail and one smooshed ear. Reward.

She had four dollars and seventy-three cents in her cat bank, a fine reward for returning a stuffed raccoon. Putting her phone number and name at the bottom, Amber propped the completed poster against her bed. Then she started on the next one.

Her mother came home while Amber was still working. She rapped on Amber's open door. "Hi, sweetie. Justin said you were in here. What are you doing?"

"Making fliers." Amber lettered her name on the last poster.

Her mother stooped to pick up one. "What a great idea. People are bound to stop and read these. If anyone has seen R.C., they will surely call you."

"I hope so."

Mrs. Cantrell sat down on Amber's bed. "Justin told me you didn't make the soccer team. I'm sorry."

"It's okay. I don't like soccer anyway." That was true, but she would have loved to have a blue-and-white captain's shirt like Mindy's.

"There's a program at the library that starts tomorrow," her mother said. "I signed you up."

Now Amber put down her pen. "A program at the library?"

"Yes, for kids. I don't know what you do exactly—make things, probably." Her mother laughed. "And you love to make things."

"Mom . . . those programs are for little kids."

"The librarian said all ages."

"I bet it's mostly little kids. The big kids have better things to do." Like soccer practice, she thought. Or running a detective agency.

"Well, it's only for a few weeks," her mother said, rising. "It'll give you something to do."

"I *have* something to do," Amber told her. "Hunt for R.C."

Her mother paused. "Amber, just in case no one calls about R.C., why don't you let your dad buy you a new stuffed animal? Or me. We'll go shopping tomorrow when I get home. You can have two stuffed animals, if you want."

Amber stared at her. "If something happened to me, would you go out and buy another girl? Would you buy *two* girls?"

"Of course not. You're my daughter. You can't be replaced."

"Well, neither can R.C." Amber finished the final poster. The subject was settled as far as she was concerned.

Mrs. Cantrell glanced at the pile of fliers. "Tell you what. After supper, I'll help you put up your fliers."

"You will?"

"Sure. In fact, I'll make you an even better offer," her mother said. "How about we go swimming at Delight's? We can put up the posters on the way to the Wakefields'."

"All right!" Amber scrambled to her feet. "I haven't gone swimming in Delight's pool yet. Wait till you see it, Mom. It's huge!"

"Sounds heavenly," Mrs. Cantrell said, going out

into the hall and picking up the mail. "A private pool, without the hassle at the community pool. I'm not sure what Irene's plans were this evening. Call Delight and ask if her parents are going out."

Amber ran into the kitchen and dialed the Wakefields' number.

Delight answered on the second ring. "Hello," she said. Her voice sounded croaky, as if she'd been crying.

"Hi, Delight. It's me, Amber. My mom and I would like to come over this evening and go swimming. If it's all right. I mean, if your parents aren't going out."

There was such a long pause, Amber thought Delight had hung up.

At last Delight said dully, "My mom will be here."

"Well, will it be okay for us to come over or not?" Earlier that day, Delight had practically begged Amber to go swimming. Now she was acting as if she could care less. What was wrong with her?

Without enthusiasm, Delight said, "Yeah, it'll be okay. Come on over."

"See you later." Amber hung up and skipped back to the living room.

Bills and advertisements lay scattered around her mother's chair. Her mother was reading a letter. She didn't look up when Amber came in.

"Delight says her mom will be home this evening," Amber reported. "So it's okay for us to go."

"Go where?" Mrs. Cantrell asked absently.

"To *Delight's,* to go swimming!" Amber put her hands on her hips, annoyed. What was the matter with people lately? First Delight was acting weird, and now her mother.

"If we're going swimming, we'll have a quick supper then." Her mother stood. The letter fell to the floor.

Amber bent to pick it up, but her mother was quicker. Mrs. Cantrell stuffed the letter in her pocket. Her mother obviously didn't want her to see it. That made Amber even more curious. Who was her mother getting secret mail from?

The phone rang. Usually Amber or Justin answered it. Justin was out, so Amber headed for the wall phone in the kitchen. But her mother beat her to it. Amber didn't realize her mother could run so fast.

"I've got it." Her mother waved Amber away. Then she turned toward the wall and spoke in a low voice.

First a secret letter and now a secret phone call. Amber wondered if the letter and call were both from her father. Maybe her mother and father were dating again, secretly.

She ran to her room to get her detective notebook. Billie Bradley wouldn't miss such an opportunity.

But when she hurried back to the kitchen with her notebook, ready to write down clues, her mother was replacing the receiver. She had a dreamy expression on her face.

Amber wrote in her notebook, *Mom looks funny*. This was definitely a clue. No doubt about it, her mother was keeping a secret.

After supper, Amber and her mother walked to the Wakefields' house. They wore bathing suits under their shorts and T-shirts. Along the way, they taped Amber's fliers to stop signs.

Mrs. Wakefield greeted them at the door. "Hi. Come on in." She led the way through the house to the patio doors.

When Amber's mother saw the pool sitting in the middle of the backyard, she exclaimed, "Irene, I had no idea it was so big!"

"It took the pool people all evening to set it up," Mrs. Wakefield said. "I'm as nervous as a cat over it. Delight's a good swimmer, but I don't know about the kids in the neighborhood. We put a stronger lock on the gate."

"Amber's a good swimmer, too," Mrs. Cantrell said. "But I've given her strict orders not to swim unless you or Mrs. Figley are around."

They all went outside.

Delight was already in the pool, paddling around on an air mattress. "Come on in, the water's great!"

Amber pulled off her shorts and T-shirt and jumped into the pool. The cool water made her shriek with laughter. She splashed a while, then climbed on the air mattress with Delight.

"Guess what?" she said.

"What?"

"I have a suspect in the case of the missing raccoon." She spoke in a solemn tone. Then she wondered if it was wise to admit her suspicions about Mindy. Billie Bradley never revealed the names of her suspects until the last few pages of the book.

Delight rolled over on her stomach. "Who?"

"I can't tell you."

"Then don't." Delight seemed peeved for some reason.

"I wish I could tell you, but I can't," Amber said hastily. "I could tell you something else though."

"Are you going to really tell me or pretend to tell me?"

"Really tell you." Amber lowered her voice. "It's about my mom. I think she's getting secret mail from my dad. I bet they're getting back together."

But Delight wasn't listening. She stared blankly into the turquoise water.

Amber didn't feel like talking either. The water lapped against the rounded sides, rocking the mattress like a cradle. She dipped her fingers into the water, trailing them dreamily.

"This is so neat," she murmured. "You can go swimming whenever you like. What a great present. You're so lucky to have a father like yours."

Delight didn't reply.

Nodding toward the patio, Amber asked, "Where is your dad, anyway?"

"At work, I guess. What do you care?"

"I just thought he'd be home so he could go swimming, that's all." Amber had never seen Delight so touchy.

Delight sat up suddenly, nearly knocking them both off the float. "I want to go in now," she said. "I'm cold."

Amber clung to the raft. "I'm not cold."

"Well, you can stay. But I'm going in."

With that, Delight heaved herself off the air mattress and climbed out of the pool. She went inside the house, leaving Amber staring after her.

What was the matter with Delight? She was acting as if she didn't want to be around Amber. Could Mindy have turned Delight against Amber? But Mindy wasn't like that. She always wanted the three of them to be friends.

But Delight was definitely acting guilty. What could she have to feel guilty about?

And then it came to her. Delight could be feeling guilty because she took something that didn't belong to her. Like a stuffed raccoon. Delight easily could have stolen R.C. from the swing.

When she got home, Amber would add a new name to her list. Delight Wakefield was suspect Number Two.

Chapter

SEVEN

The library was near the shopping center where Amber's mother bought groceries. Justin and Amber rode the bus there. While Amber was in her program, Justin planned to browse through car magazines.

"Afterward," he said, "we can walk over to the shopping center and get frozen yogurt."

"I don't really want to go to this thing," Amber admitted, as they got off the bus. "Mom thinks I'm lonely on the days Mindy and Delight have soccer. But I'd rather be looking for R.C."

"Amber," Justin said, leading the way up the flagstone walk, "R.C.'s been gone for days. Do you really think you'll ever get him back?"

"Yes, I do. R.C. is out there somewhere, waiting for me to find him."

Justin rolled his eyes as he opened the glass door. "You're nuttier than I thought!"

His remark made Amber more anxious than ever to resume her search. She would catch the raccoon-napper and show Justin and everyone else they were wrong. Going to the library program was just a waste of time.

In the library, Amber walked into the bright, sunny children's room. Her heart sank.

Sitting around the tables were children no older than first-graders. Mindy's little sister Karen was there, holding a large paper bag. Many kids had brought snacks, Amber noticed. That meant it was a long program.

She waved to Karen, who nervously waved back. When the librarian asked them all to settle down, Karen stowed the bag under her chair.

The librarian was named Miss Marsh. She smiled at Amber, who hung back, and indicated she should join the others.

"Let's make a nice, big group," said Miss Marsh.

Amber perched on one of the small chairs. The little kids stared at her. She felt ridiculous. If only her mother hadn't signed her up for this dumb program!

Miss Marsh checked off names on her list, then assembled supplies for the craft project.

"We're going to make birds today," she said, doling out macaroni, pipe cleaners, glue, paper, and feathers to each child.

Amber scowled at the allotment of macaroni and feathers she'd been given. This project was way beneath her.

Miss Marsh came over. "Some of the things I've planned for this program might be boring for you," she apologized. "Would you like to be my assistant instead? I could really use your help, Amber."

"What would I have to do?"

"Pick up books the children scatter around. Be in charge of the supplies. Maybe help me read a story . . . don't worry, there's lots to do." She smiled. "When we're not busy, you can choose books to check out."

This didn't sound too bad. Amber liked the idea of being the librarian's assistant.

"Do you know the Billie Bradley books?" she asked.

"Oh, yes. They're very popular. Can't keep them on the shelf." Miss Marsh rummaged through a cart. "Here's the latest Billie Bradley mystery. I was about to shelve it, but you can be the first to check it out. In fact, I'll reserve new Billie Bradley books for you as they come in."

Amber's heart leaped with joy. A new Billie Bradley book! Suddenly she was glad her mother had signed her up for the program.

"I'll be glad to be your assistant," she said. "I even know one of the kids. I'll go see if she needs any help. You know how little kids are with glue."

She walked over to where Karen Alexander was sitting. Karen's macaroni bird was a mess. She had glued the tail feathers on upside-down.

"Hi, Karen," Amber said.

Karen regarded her through narrow eyes. "Hi. How come you're here? You're too big."

"I'm Miss Marsh's assistant. Here, let me show you how to fix your bird."

"No!" Karen covered her project with her arms. "I like it the way it is."

Amber shrugged. "Okay. I'll leave you alone then."

She moved on to a little boy who was eating his macaroni. Karen probably felt uncomfortable being singled out by the librarian's assistant. That was why she seemed so jittery. Next time, she'd wait until Karen asked for help.

When Justin came by half an hour later, Amber proudly announced she was the librarian's assistant. That was better than being a soccer team captain any day.

Amber skipped across Carriage Street to Mindy's house. It was Saturday. Amber's father was coming from Maryland to pick up her and Justin. They were going to spend the day doing all sorts of neat things. First, they would go to a movie, then shopping, and later to a concert in the park.

Amber couldn't wait to tell Mindy about her outing. She rapped on the Alexanders' front door, humming a song.

Mrs. Alexander came to the door, carrying Sarah. "Hi, Amber."

"Hi, Mrs. Alexander. Hi, Sarah." Sarah smiled gummily at her. "Is Mindy here?" Amber asked.

Mrs. Alexander shook her head. "No, she and Karen went to Delight's to go swimming. I think they're planning to stay over there nearly the whole day."

Amber felt a jab of jealousy. Mindy was certainly spending a lot of time at Delight's house lately. And she hadn't bothered telling her best-best friend either.

"Well, let Mindy know I was here," Amber said.

"I will." Mrs. Alexander shut the door.

Amber walked slowly across Carriage Street. Then she saw her father's car turn the corner. Breaking into a run, she hurried to greet him. Let Delight and Mindy play in that stale old swimming pool.

"Daddy!" Amber cried as her father pulled into the driveway.

"Hello, pumpkin," her father said, leaning out the window. "Are you and Justin ready to roll? We've got a big day ahead."

At that moment, Justin came out, followed by Mrs. Cantrell.

"I'll have the kids home before dark," Mr.

Cantrell promised her. "I might even feed them. But only a crust of bread."

"Oh, Daddy, you're so funny." Amber giggled as she climbed into the backseat.

She watched intently as her father and mother said good-bye. They seemed more like friends than like people who were secretly dating. Still, she thought, her parents could be very good actors.

Pulling out her notebook, she wrote, *Mom and Dad are nice to each other.*

They drove to the mall first and had lunch at Amber's favorite pizza place. Justin and Mr. Cantrell discussed a baseball game they'd seen on TV the night before.

After lunch, they went into the movie theater. Even though they'd just eaten, Mr. Cantrell splurged and bought Justin and Amber a bucket of popcorn to share. The movie was funny. Amber laughed so much, her sides hurt.

When they came out of the theater, Mr. Cantrell suggested they walk around the mall before leaving for the park.

Amber tucked her hand in her father's. "This is so much fun," she said happily. "I wish we could do this every weekend. Every *day,* even! I love summer!"

"You'd get bored if you did this every single day," her father said.

"Not me!" She skipped ahead to stick her fingers

in the fountain.

When she skipped back again, she found her father and brother deep in conversation. Then she heard her father say "Philadelphia" and her heart sank. She knew what they were talking about.

The lady friend her father used to see lived in Philadelphia. Her father must be planning to visit her again. As long as her parents weren't dating other people, there was the possibility they would get back together. But now her father was going to wreck everything.

She ran up to him. "You aren't going up to Philadelphia again, are you?" she said accusingly.

Mr. Cantrell smiled. "Yes, I am. I'm going to see Ruth."

"And that kid Jessica!" The lady in Philadelphia had a daughter Amber's age.

Her father looked surprised. "Amber, what is the matter with you?"

Justin answered, "She's been nuts ever since she lost that dumb raccoon."

"You haven't found him yet?" Mr. Cantrell asked Amber.

She shook her head. "I didn't lose him! I put him on the swing and went in the house for a second. When I came out, he was gone." Tears threatened to spill down her cheeks. Her happy summer feeling vanished.

"Have you looked everywhere?" her father asked.

"I've looked but I can't find him." Rubbing her eyes with her fists, she added miserably, "R.C. is gone and now you're going out with that lady again! How can you and Mom get back together if you're in Philadelphia?"

Her father put his arm around her. "Amber, I'm sorry you're upset because I want to visit Ruth. But your mother and I are just good friends. We are both seeing other people."

This news made Amber gasp. Suddenly she understood the meaning of the letter her mother didn't want her to see. And the mysterious phone call. They weren't from her father, but from some other man.

She whirled on her brother. "Do you know about this? About Mom?"

"Of course," Justin replied.

Amber burst into tears. She didn't care that they were standing in the middle of the mall. She didn't care that people were staring at her.

"Amber, don't cry." Her father led her to a bench. "Nothing will change between us. We are still a family. We just don't happen to live in the same house."

But things *were* changing. Her mother was getting letters and phone calls from a man. Her father was going to see that lady in Philadelphia again. Her best-best friend was spending more time with Delight than with Amber. Worst of all, she couldn't find R.C.

"It's that stuffed animal," Justin said to Mr. Cantrell. "She hasn't been the same since it disappeared."

Mr. Cantrell patted Amber's shoulder. "Well, maybe we can fix that." He pointed to a toy store. "Let's see if we can find another R.C."

"I don't want another R.C.," Amber sniffed. "I want my *old* R.C." But she followed her father into the toy store anyway.

The shelves were crammed with a zoo of stuffed animals. There were parrots and tigers and giraffes. There was even a stuffed penguin, like Mindy's. But no stuffed raccoons.

"How about something different?" Mr. Cantrell suggested, pulling a shaggy-maned lion off the shelf. "How about this guy? He has a real leather collar." He made the lion growl.

Amber refused to consider the lion. She was loyal to one stuffed animal. She couldn't be swayed by any fancy leather collar.

"I don't want a lion," she said stubbornly. "I want my raccoon. I want R.C.!"

Her father sighed. "If you don't want any of these other stuffed animals, then we'll go to the park. The concert will be starting soon. How about if we get ice cream afterward? Does that sound good?"

Nothing sounded good to Amber now. She didn't care about the concert or ice cream. Her summer feeling was gone forever, like R.C.

She wondered if she would ever be happy again.

When her father's car stopped in front of Amber's house, Amber jumped out.

"Good-bye," she told her father. To her mother, who was coming down the walk, she said, "I'm going to Mindy's." She couldn't wait to tell her best-best friend about her horrible day.

Mrs. Alexander let her in, saying that Mindy was in her bedroom.

As Amber headed down the hall, Mindy's sister Karen yelled, "Amber's coming!" It sounded like a warning to Amber.

At once Mindy appeared in the doorway of her bedroom. She looked flushed.

"What are you doing here?" she said, slamming her bedroom door shut behind her. She stood in front of the door like a guard.

Amber was surprised at her friend's rude behavior. "I came over to see you. I haven't seen you all day. You were at Delight's when I came by this morning," she added testily.

"Well, you were going away with your father," Mindy said, equally testy.

"How come we're standing in the hall?" asked

Amber. "Can't we go in your room?"

Mindy jiggled the doorknob, as if to make sure it was firmly closed. "No. It's a mess."

"I've seen messy rooms before."

"Not like this. You can't even walk. In fact, I have to clean it up this evening."

"I'll help you." Amber didn't really want to help clean Mindy's room, but she needed to talk to somebody.

"No!" Mindy said quickly. "I mean, my mom said I have to clean it up all by myself." She shrugged apologetically.

Amber didn't need Mindy to draw her a picture. Obviously she didn't want Amber around. Turning, Amber stalked back down the hall.

"See you tomorrow?" Mindy called after her.

Amber didn't reply.

Leaving Mindy's house, she walked up Carriage Street toward Little Rocky Run. All the while, her brain was buzzing.

Mindy seemed to be covering up something. She definitely didn't want Amber in her room. What was she hiding? A stolen raccoon?

Or maybe Mindy didn't want to be friends anymore. Maybe Mindy wanted to be best friends with Delight now. This thought bothered Amber even more than the idea that Mindy had taken R.C.

Her worries kept her occupied across the bridge

and up the hill. Soon she was standing in front of Delight's house. The gate stood open. Amber went into the backyard.

Delight sat alone on the patio, wrapped in a pink-striped beach towel. The beautiful new pool was empty.

"Hi," Amber said.

Delight glanced around. "Hi. When did you get back?"

"A little while ago." She flopped down in the chair opposite Delight.

"Did you have a good time?"

"No," Amber said, glad she could finally spill her troubles to somebody. "It was awful. I found out my father is dating that lady in Philadelphia again. You know, the one with the kid named Jessica? And my mother is getting letters and phone calls from a man." She slumped in her seat. "They'll never get back together at this rate."

To Amber's amazement, Delight began to cry.

Amber was touched by Delight's concern. "It's okay, really. I'm getting used to them being divorced. I just thought that they'd get back together someday."

Delight cried even harder.

"Gee, I don't feel as bad as you do," Amber said.

"It's not that," Delight sobbed. "It's—"

"What?" Amber leaned forward eagerly. Was Delight about to reveal her secret?

Her shoulders shaking, Delight struggled to stop crying. Finally she said, "My parents are getting divorced. Just like yours!"

Amber didn't know what to say. She watched Delight cry into the beach towel a moment, then asked hesitantly, "Are you sure? I mean, did your parents tell you they're getting divorced?"

Delight wiped her eyes. "Mom told me she and Dad are separating. Dad's going to go live someplace else. I know what that means. They'll get divorced."

Amber nodded. "That's kind of the way it happened to my parents. My dad moved out first. Then after a while, Mom told me they were getting a divorce. And they did."

"See? It always happens that way."

"Maybe it won't be too bad," Amber said consolingly. "Your dad got you that pool—"

"I don't care about the stupid pool," Delight said bitterly. "I want my dad back." Fresh tears filled her red-rimmed eyes. "You know what else my mom said?"

Amber shook her head.

"We might have to move. My mom isn't sure we can keep the house. It's too big or expensive or something."

Amber felt strangely happy at this news. If Delight moved away, Amber would rule the neighborhood. Mindy would spend more time with

Amber, like she used to before Delight came.

"Where will you move to?" she asked.

"I don't know." Delight looked around, as if memorizing her backyard. "I like it here. This is the best place we've ever lived. I'm sick of moving. I'd have to leave my friends—"

"You'll make new ones." Amber remembered how quickly Delight had made friends in their third grade class.

Delight's face crumpled again. "I don't want to make new friends! I want to stay here so I can play with you and Mindy and David and even that horrible Henry Hoffstedder. Why does this have to happen?"

Amber didn't have an answer for that. Tears stung her eyes as she recalled that awful day when her own father had left. From the porch stoop, she had watched him carry suits and shirts out to his car. Then he drove away. Amber had never felt so sad.

"It's not fair," Delight sobbed.

"No," Amber replied. She was crying, too. "It isn't."

She felt a pang of guilt. A few seconds ago she was glad to be queen of the neighborhood, glad to have Delight out of the way. How could she think about being popular when one of her best friends was so unhappy?

She pushed her chair closer to Delight's. They didn't talk, but sat quietly in the gathering twilight, as fireflies blinked in the honeysuckle.

EIGHT

During the next week, Amber received three stuffed animals: a pink panda from her father, a colorful parrot from her mother, and a dinosaur from Justin.

Amber was touched by the presents, especially the dinosaur from Justin. He had spent his baby-sitting money on it. The stuffed animals were cute, but they weren't R.C. She lined them up on her bookshelf. None of the newcomers belonged on her bed. That spot was reserved for R.C.

No one called in response to her fliers.

The Carriage Street Crime-Busters met every day. R.C. had been missing for nearly three weeks, but they hadn't turned up a single clue.

One morning, while Amber and Delight were waiting for Mindy, Delight told Amber that her father was looking for an apartment.

"As soon as he finds one he likes, I guess he'll move out," Delight said.

"You'll still see him," Amber said. "My dad and mom say we're still a family, even though we don't live in the same house."

Delight had no comment. Amber knew she found it hard to believe that a family who didn't live together was still a family.

"Have you told Mindy about this?" Amber asked.

"No. Only you."

Amber was surprised. "Only me? But Mindy's your friend, too."

"I don't think Mindy would understand," Delight explained. "But you know what it's like."

Amber felt pleased that Delight had chosen her to confide in. "I won't tell anyone," she promised. "Not even Mindy." Still, it wouldn't be easy keeping a secret this big from her best-best friend.

Just then Mindy ran across the street.

"Sorry I'm late, guys. I had to play with Sarah while Mom vacuumed." She flopped down on the grass. "What's up today?"

Amber had brought out her detective box. She kept her notebook buried at the bottom, out of sight. It would be awful if Mindy or Delight saw it and learned they were Amber's main suspects.

She didn't want to believe her two closest friends

might have taken her most prized possession in the world. But so far, Mindy and Delight were the only ones who'd been acting strangely since R.C.'s disappearance.

"We've combed the neighborhood," Amber said with a sigh. "And we haven't found a thing."

"I found a quarter," Delight corrected.

Amber looked at her.

"Well, it was *something*. Anyway, I put it in our treasury, didn't I? I could have spent it on myself."

"It's so weird," Mindy remarked. "It's like a giant hand came down from the sky and grabbed R.C."

Amber often had the same thought. She wondered if Billie Bradley had ever had such a tough case. Then she realized that in all the Billie Bradley books, people came to *her* with mysteries to be solved. Nothing ever happened to Billie Bradley herself.

Amber tried to imagine what Billie Bradley would do if something of hers was stolen. She squeezed her eyes shut and concentrated. Billie Bradley would probably question people who might have seen something suspicious.

She thought back to the day R.C. vanished. She was in the house, helping her mother put away groceries. Someone in the neighborhood could have easily witnessed the crime.

Suddenly Amber's eyes flew open. Of course! Mindy was the obvious person to question. After all, she lived right across the street.

"Mindy," Amber asked. "Remember the day I lost R.C.?"

"No."

"It was the first day of summer vacation," Amber reminded her. "We formed our detective agency that day, remember?"

"And followed David and Henry to the creek," Delight put in.

"Yeah," Amber said quickly before anyone could bring up that embarrassing incident with the snake.

"I remember now," Mindy said. "What about that day?"

"We all went home that afternoon," Amber said. "I sat on the patio with R.C. Then I went inside the house. When I came out, R.C. was gone. Mindy, did you look out your window? Did you happen to see anybody hanging around my house?"

Mindy frowned. "No, I didn't see anybody— wait!"

Amber leaned forward eagerly. Billie Bradley's technique worked! "What did you see?"

"I was playing ball with Karen that day and I saw a man walk by," Mindy said excitedly.

"What man? Did you know him?"

"Well, it sort of looked like Mr. Anderson," Mindy said. "You know, that slow way he walks."

"Mr. Anderson," Delight repeated. "Who's he?"

"He lives down the street," Amber said. "He gives out money on Halloween."

"You don't think *he* took R.C.?"

Amber couldn't imagine why an old man would steal a stuffed raccoon. But it was better than thinking her best-best friend did it.

"We have to follow every lead," she said, getting up. "Come on, Crime-Busters. Let's go."

Mr. Anderson lived in a white house with black shutters. Red geraniums bloomed cheerfully along his walk. It didn't look like the house of a raccoon-napper. His small car was parked in the driveway.

"He's home," Amber whispered. "Get down, everybody. He might be armed and dangerous."

They crept along the side of his house, sheltered by pungent-smelling bushes. Carefully they rose up to peer in the nearest window. They looked into a room with a wooden table and chairs.

"Dining room," Amber whispered. "Let's try a back window."

They edged around the house, still camouflaged by the thick bushes. The next window they peeked in showed a stove. The suspect himself was sitting at the kitchen counter.

"He's sharpening his knife," Amber said. "He's the culprit, all right!"

"Amber, he's buttering a slice of bread," Delight observed.

Amber was sure she had found the raccoon-napper. "When he's done with it, I bet he uses it as a weapon."

Mindy shook her head. "Amber I don't think he took your raccoon. He's too nice."

"That's all an act. He acts nice just to fool people."

Delight seemed unconvinced, too. "I think we're way off base. He looks perfectly innocent to me."

"He's a criminal!" Amber insisted. The scent from the bushes tickled her nose. Suddenly she sneezed so hard, she bumped her forehead against the window.

Mr. Anderson heard the noise and looked in their direction. They'd been spotted!

Horrified, Amber watched as the desperate criminal got up and opened the back door.

"Amber?" he called. "Amber Cantrell? Is that you?"

It was too late to run. He had them.

"Yes," Amber confessed. "It's me. And Mindy and Delight."

"What are you doing in there?" Mr. Anderson asked when they crawled out of his bushes.

"I lost something," Amber said weakly. Well, she *had*. "I thought it might be here."

Mr. Anderson appeared concerned. "That's too bad. Maybe I can help you find it. What is it?"

"A stuffed raccoon," Mindy replied. "You haven't seen one around, have you?"

He tried to hide a smile. "No, I can't say I have. But if I see one, I'll let you know."

The Carriage Street Crime-Busters left Mr. Anderson's yard. Amber's shoulders slumped dejectedly. The only lead had proved to be false. Would she ever find R.C.?

At home, she found Justin hanging up the phone. "That was Mom. She called to say she's going out later."

"Where is she going?" Amber asked. Her mother hardly ever went anywhere, except to work or to run errands.

"I think she's going out to dinner with this guy who buys a lot of stuff from her shop."

"I don't like this," Amber said. "I wish things would stay the same."

Justin shrugged. "Nothing does."

She was afraid he was right.

When her mother came home later, Amber didn't go out to meet her as she usually did.

Mrs. Cantrell knocked on Amber's door. "Hi, sweetie."

Amber stared at her book.

Her mother sighed. "I know why you're upset. It's because I'm going out tonight. I'm going to dinner with a man named Phillip. He comes into the shop regularly. He's very nice."

"I don't like it," Amber said.

"I know it's hard. It's hard for me, too," her mother admitted. "Phillip has been asking me out for months and I've only just now accepted. I was worried about how you and Justin would feel." Her mother waited for Amber to say something, then left to change.

Amber knew she shouldn't act this way. Her mother didn't have very much fun.

Mrs. Cantrell came back into Amber's room, wearing a red dress and sandals.

"Is this outfit all right?" she asked Amber. "You don't think it's too much?"

"You look terrific, Mom." She smiled. "Really."

Her mother swooped to kiss her. "Thanks, sweetie. I brought home baked chicken for dinner. Justin is fixing French fries."

After supper, Justin and Amber made popcorn and watched TV until it was time for Amber to go to bed. A short time later, she heard Justin go into his room. Her mother still wasn't back from her date.

Amber tried to sleep, but her room was stuffy. She padded out to the living room and curled up on the couch. Moonlight poured through the picture window. Amber thought about everything that had happened so far this summer.

The worst, she decided, was that she had lost R.C. If her raccoon was there to hug, the other problems wouldn't be so bad.

A key turned in the lock on the front door.

Mrs. Cantrell entered, surprised to see Amber. She switched on a lamp. "Amber, why are you up? Are you sick?"

"No, I just can't sleep."

Her mother sat beside her. "Were you worried about my date?"

"A little," Amber said. "I wish things would stay the same. This isn't the fun summer I thought it would be. Delight told me her parents are getting a divorce. It's sad, isn't it?"

"Yes, it is." Her mother drew her closer. "Amber, your father and I love you and Justin very much. That didn't change when we divorced."

"I know," Amber said. "It's just that—"

"What?"

"I want my raccoon back." Tears streamed down her cheeks. Her heart ached from missing R.C. What would she do if she never got him back?

Her mother held her until she stopped crying, then walked her back to bed and tucked her in. "It'll be okay, Amber. You'll see."

But Amber didn't think anything would be okay ever again.

The next day, Amber met Mindy and Delight after their soccer game.

"We lost," Mindy reported glumly.

"You'll win next time," Amber said as they crossed the bridge over the creek. "Let's go wading."

Eagerly, the girls walked down to the water's edge. They took off their sneakers and waded in the cool water, shrieking when they slipped on moss-slicked rocks.

Amber waded to the bank. She began arranging pebbles in little groups. The others came over to watch.

"This is our neighborhood," she said. "Our houses will be here forever. Here's my house."

Mindy added a pebble near Amber's pebble. "And here's mine."

With a stick, Amber drew a squiggly line. "This is the creek."

"Now put in your house," Mindy said to Delight. "That's your side of the neighborhood."

Delight picked up a smooth white stone and held it loosely between two fingers. She looked at Amber's and Mindy's pebble houses, then threw her pebble down. Grabbing her sneakers, she ran up the bank and over the bridge toward Amber's house.

"Delight!" Amber shouted. "Come back!"

"What's wrong with her?" Mindy asked Amber.

Amber knew, but she couldn't say.

Mindy stared at her. "You know, don't you? You know what's wrong with Delight. How come you won't tell me?"

"I can't." Amber spread her hands helplessly.

"But we're best friends!"

"I still can't tell you. I promised."

Mindy snatched up her sneakers. "All right, if that's the way you want it! Be Delight's best friend, see if I care!" She scrambled up the bank.

Amber looked down at the pebble neighborhood. With her bare foot, she scattered the pebbles. Then she went home.

Mindy and Delight were in Mindy's yard. Mindy turned away when she saw Amber.

Let her be like that, Amber thought. Then she spied an object on her front stoop. It was a rock with a piece of paper taped to it. Her name was printed on the tape.

Pulling off the paper, she smoothed it on the cement. One sentence was sloppily printed on the paper:

I've got your raccoon.

It was a message from the raccoon-napper!

Amber's hands trembled with excitement. "Mindy! Delight!" she cried. "Come here!"

"What is it?" Delight called, running across the street. Mindy ran behind her.

"It's a note from the raccoon-napper! I finally heard from him. Or her."

Then Amber remembered that Billie Bradley never showed any surprise when she found a clue. Billie Bradley was always a professional detective.

"Let's go in the lab," Amber said. "We have to analyze the clue."

"What lab?" asked Mindy.

"My room," Amber informed them, "is also a lab."

With the magnifying glass, Amber studied the

note. There was something odd about the way the raccoon-napper had printed the *o*'s.

"He's not a very good writer," Mindy observed.

"Yeah. Look at the *o*'s," Amber said.

Delight bent over the note. "They're flat. They're supposed to be round."

Mindy sat back on her heels. "Who do we know who makes their *o*'s like that?"

Amber shook her head. "I don't know. But this is our first real clue. We can ask suspects to write something and see if they make their *o*'s the same."

"Maybe the raccoon-napper will send another note," said Delight.

"They always do," Mindy said. "Next time he'll probably ask for money."

Amber narrowed her eyes at Mindy. Her best friend seemed to know an awful lot about the way criminals behaved. "How do you know it's a he?"

"I don't. It could be a she."

Yes, it could, thought Amber. Mindy had had plenty of time to put the rock on Amber's stoop after running away from the creek. So had Delight, for that matter. But Delight's peculiar behavior had an explanation. She was upset because her parents were separating. Mindy didn't have an excuse.

"I have to go," Delight said. "Mrs. Figley has an appointment and I have to go with her."

When Delight left, Amber expected Mindy to

apologize for blowing up. But she said, "I have to go, too."

"You have an appointment, too?" Amber asked tartly.

Mindy was already halfway across the street. "Maybe."

So Mindy was still mad at her. The appearance of the first real clue in the case of the missing raccoon wasn't enough to make Mindy forget about their fight.

The next morning, Amber walked up the hill to find Delight sitting by her pool. She was hugging Row-bear, her French stuffed dog.

"My dad moved out last night," Delight announced to Amber.

Amber plopped down next to her. "Where did he go?"

"To an apartment not too far away. He took me over there. It's nice, I guess."

"Will you have to move now?" Amber asked. Panic gripped her stomach. Mindy was acting really weird. If Delight moved, Amber wouldn't have any friends at all.

"Mom says we'll have to see. Whatever that means." She sighed. "I don't know why my parents can't live in the same house anymore."

"It doesn't make much sense," Amber agreed. "When I grow up, I'm not ever going to get a divorce."

"I'm not even getting married."

Amber tried to make her laugh. "Somebody has to ask you first. Suppose it's Henry Hoffstedder?"

"Ewww! No way would I marry Henry!" Delight giggled.

"Me neither!"

"Where's Mindy?" Delight asked.

"We had a fight yesterday," Amber explained. "She didn't tell you?"

Delight shook her head.

"Mindy knows you told me a secret and she got mad. But I didn't say anything about—you know," Amber said.

"I should tell her. But Mindy's not like us. She wouldn't understand."

Amber recalled the time her father had moved out. Mindy became Amber's best friend that summer. She didn't have to tell Mindy how she felt—somehow Mindy understood.

"I think she will," Amber told Delight. "But it's up to you. I know how it is. You think people will feel sorry for you and you don't want that."

"I'm glad I can talk to you," Delight said. She placed Row-bear on the ground between them. "Row-bear will belong to both of us. We can share him until R.C. comes back."

The Fourth of July weekend was approaching. Justin's birthday was on the fifth of July. Mrs. Cantrell planned a cookout to combine the two events.

"We'll have hamburgers and hot dogs and potato salad and corn on the cob. An old-fashioned barbecue," she told Amber. "I'm inviting Irene Wakefield, and Delight, of course. Irene is having a rough time. She could use a little fun."

"So could Delight," Amber said. "Are you asking Mindy and her mom?"

"Naturally." Mrs. Cantrell didn't know that Amber and Mindy had argued. "And Justin gets to invite whomever he wants."

"Gee, thanks," Justin said sarcastically. "I was beginning to think this wasn't my birthday."

"Can we have fireworks?" Amber wanted to know.

She loved the Fourth of July. Bunting-draped stands had already sprung up on street corners, filled with exciting items like Roman candles, Yankee Doodles, and the enormous, expensive Rocket to Jupiter.

Mrs. Cantrell frowned. Although fireworks were legal in Virginia, she didn't like them. "Only sparklers," she said. "The others are too dangerous or too noisy."

Mr. Cantrell was going to be away the weekend of the birthday barbecue, but he took Justin to an Orioles game. When he dropped Justin off after the game, he came into Amber's room to visit her.

He saw the collection of new stuffed animals lined up neatly on her bookshelf.

"Wow," he exclaimed. "It looks like a stuffed animal convention. They should all be wearing little name tags that say 'Hello, my name is so-and-so.' "

Amber smiled. "They're all cute. I like the one you gave me . . ."

"But . . ." Her father prompted her to finish her sentence.

"They aren't R.C." She found herself spilling her troubles: her fight with Mindy, her fear that Delight would have to move away, her suspicions that Mindy might have stolen R.C.

"I get so lonely at night without R.C.," she concluded miserably.

Her father sat on the bed, his weight denting the mattress. "Close your eyes," he said. "Tell me what R.C. looks like. Can you see him?"

"Oh, yes," Amber replied. "He's sitting on my pillow, like always. He has one smooshed ear. And the fur on his face is worn off a little." She opened her eyes. "Only he's not here."

"Not on your pillow," her father said gently. "But he's in your memory, isn't he? You will always remember R.C. No one can take those memories away from you."

"I guess not."

Her father put his arm around her. "You know what I liked most about R.C.?"

"What?"

"He was loyal. He was the most loyal raccoon in the world. And you know what else?"

Amber leaned against her father. "What else?"

"You are just as loyal as R.C. Maybe even more loyal."

"How am I loyal?" She liked hearing nice things about herself.

Her father's voice rumbled soothingly. "You're loyal to your friends. You're helping Delight get through a rough time. And you're worried about Mindy, even though you suspect she might have taken R.C. That's real loyalty."

"Do you think I'll make it without R.C.?"

He hugged her tightly. "Yes, indeed. You are very brave, Amber Gillian Cantrell."

His praise made her feel good. Maybe her father was right. Maybe she *could* get along without R.C.

But she didn't feel like being brave. All the bad things seemed to happen after R.C. vanished. If her raccoon came back, would everything be wonderful again?

The Fourth of July was hot and sunny. Justin and Amber helped their mother get ready for the cookout.

Justin loaded an old red wagon with ice and filled it with canned sodas. Amber arranged napkins, paper plates, and plastic cups in a large basket, while Mrs.

Cantrell cleaned the grill.

Mindy and her mother were the first guests. Mrs. Alexander handed Justin a bandanna-wrapped present.

"Thanks, Mrs. Alexander," Justin said, opening the bandanna to reveal a cassette tape he'd been wanting. He tied the bandanna around his forehead, pirate-style.

Mindy perched on the swing. She greeted Amber coolly.

Amber went into the house and brought out bowls of potato chips and corn chips. She set them primly on the patio table. Then, tired of playing Mindy's game, she walked over to the swing with one of the snack bowls and said, "Chip?"

Mindy took a potato chip and ate it.

"Are you going to be mad at me forever?" Amber demanded.

"I'm not mad at you."

This was certainly news to Amber. "Then how come you're always busy when I go over to your house?"

"I am busy," Mindy said.

Amber was dying to know what mysterious project was keeping Mindy so busy. Could it have something to do with R.C.? But she wouldn't ask. Mindy would have to tell her herself.

"You haven't been lonesome," Mindy pointed out. "You've been playing with Delight Wakefield."

"How do you know?"

"I see you walking up the hill. I guess you and Delight go swimming and talk about things." Mindy was hinting heavily, but Amber wouldn't give away Delight's secret.

Justin's friends arrived in a noisy group. Then Delight and her mother came. Mrs. Wakefield also gave Justin a cassette tape.

"Great. Now I've got two new tapes," he said, slipping one into his cassette player. Thumping music crashed over the lawn. Mrs. Cantrell made him turn it down.

Soon hot dogs and hamburgers were sizzling on the grill. The boys had a potato chip fight. The girls went under a shade tree to get out of the way.

Mindy sat a little apart from Delight and Amber. Amber knew she was still miffed.

Delight seemed to sense it, too.

"I guess I should tell you, Mindy," she said quietly. "My parents are getting a divorce."

Mindy's eyes widened. "Really?"

"Yes, really. My dad moved to an apartment." Delight sketched aimless circles in the mulch around the base of the tree. "There's something else. My mom and I might have to move, too. She doesn't know if she can keep the house."

"Oh, no," Mindy cried. "You can't move!"

"I don't want you to move either," Amber said.

"We're all best friends, aren't we?"

Delight stared at the ground. "Well, you and Mindy are best friends. Only two people can be best friends."

"Three people can be best friends," Amber stated.

"Right," agreed Mindy.

"I'm glad," said Delight. "I can be best friends with you guys until we have to move. *If* we have to move."

"Come and get it!" Mrs. Cantrell called.

The girls loaded paper plates with hamburgers, hot dogs, and all the fixings, then went back to their tree to eat.

"Hurry up and eat," Amber said. "We've got sparklers."

After they had tossed their paper plates in the garbage bag, Amber asked her mother if they could light the sparklers.

"Amber, it isn't even dark yet."

"We don't care. Can we have them now?"

Her mother went inside and brought out boxes of sparklers.

"Baby stuff," Justin said scornfully, but Amber noticed him and his friends eyeing her box of sparklers.

"You can have one," she said, handing him a wire with its thick coating at the top. Delight and Mindy shared theirs with Justin's friends.

Mrs. Cantrell helped them light the sparklers.

As soon as Amber's was fizzing, she shrieked excitedly and swooped her arm in gigantic arcs. The sparkler left a fiery trail.

"I'm writing my name!" Delight called.

"Me, too!" said Mindy. "In cursive!"

Amber tried to write *Amber Gillian Cantrell,* but by the time she reached the last two *ll*s, the first part of her name had turned to smoke.

Her sparkler was nearly out. She quickly exchanged it for a new one. Soon the girls were twirling a sparkler in each hand.

It was nearly dark when the last sparkler sputtered out.

The girls escaped to the front yard to get away from Justin's noisy friends.

Mindy picked up something lying on the walk. "What's this?"

Amber took it from her. It was a piece of paper taped to a rock. Her name was written on the tape.

Her heart pounded. "It's another note from the raccoon-napper!" she exclaimed.

"Maybe he's giving R.C. back," said Delight.

Amber stripped off the tape and flattened out the wrinkled paper. Like the first kidnap note, this one had been clumsily printed.

It read: *If you want your raccoon back, meet me at the bridge. Tomorrow at nine. Bring money.*

Mindy gave a low whistle. "Whoever this person is, he means business."

"It could be a she," Delight reminded them. "What are you going to do, Amber?"

Amber stared at the handwriting. There were those same flat-bottomed *o*'s. Suddenly she remembered where she had seen *o*'s like that before.

She knew the identity of the raccoon-napper.

Chapter TEN

I know who did it!" Amber crowed. "I know who stole R.C."

"Who?" Mindy and Delight demanded at the same time.

"I have to check something first," she told them. "Just to make sure."

"Amber!" Delight exclaimed. "Tell us!"

But Billie Bradley never revealed the identity of the culprit until she accused the suspect.

The boom of distant fireworks filled the night. It was too late to catch the raccoon-napper.

"Meet me tomorrow morning," Amber ordered. *"Early."*

After her friends had left, Amber took the note to her room. She compared the new note with the previous note tucked in her detective notebook. They had both been written by the same person.

Then she pulled out her end-of-the-year folder from under her bed. Sorting through her "A" papers, she found the paper she wanted. With the magnifying glass, she examined the note and the paper. No doubt about it, the flat-bottomed o's were identical.

She definitely knew who had written the notes. Now all she had to do was wait until the next day.

The next morning, Amber shot out of her house faster than any firecracker.

Mindy was just crossing the street and Delight was hurrying down from the corner. Amber didn't stop.

"Wait up!" Mindy cried.

Amber couldn't wait. It was bad enough she'd had to wait all night.

"Amber!" Delight yelled. "Tell us who took R.C."

But Amber had no time to talk. She sprinted up Carriage Street, across the bridge over Little Rocky Run, and up the steep hill. When she reached Buggy Whip Lane, she turned and ran directly to the third house on the left.

"This is David Jackson's house," Delight said, catching up.

"Amber," Mindy panted, "do you think David stole R.C.?"

"Not David. But a real snake!"

Amber passed by the front door, and jogged around back.

Along one edge of the yard were several cages and fish tanks. A sign proclaimed "Reptile Zoo" in the same crooked printing used in the notes Amber had received.

She bet anything he was there. And he was.

David and Henry were feeding the occupants of the cages. They looked up when they saw Amber barreling across the yard toward them. Henry dropped the can of worms he was holding.

With a warlike whoop, Amber tackled Henry Hoffstedder, knocking him flat on his back. She sat on his chest, pinning him to the ground.

"Where's R.C.?" she demanded, pummeling him with both fists. "Where's my raccoon, you dirty, rotten raccoon-napper!"

Henry couldn't talk, or even breathe, with Amber straddling his chest.

"Mmmmfff!" His face turned purple.

David grabbed Amber's shoulders and tried to pull her off.

"Amber needs help!" Mindy shouted.

She and Delight both jumped David. The three of them toppled over in a heap of arms and legs. From the bottom of the pile came a blood-curdling yell.

"LET ME UP!" roared Henry.

David, Mindy, and Delight rolled off the pile, but

Amber clung to Henry like a burr.

Henry Hoffstedder had done some pretty awful things, but this was the absolute worst. She would not give up until she had her raccoon back and Henry had apologized.

He tried to push her away. "Get off!"

Amber hung on like a bronco rider. "Not until you give me my raccoon!"

"I can't give you anything if you don't let me up!"

That made sense. Amber clambered to her feet, dragging Henry with her by the collar of his T-shirt. She wasn't about to let him go.

"All right," she said. "Now where's R.C.? What have you done with him?"

"Nothing."

"What do you mean, nothing? You took my raccoon!" Amber shook Henry like a dust mop. "Give him back to me!"

"I don't have your stupid stuffed animal!"

"You're lying, Henry Hoffstedder," Amber said through her teeth. "You sent me those notes. I recognized your crummy printing. You shouldn't have stuck that spelling paper in my school folder. That's how I knew it was you."

"Yeah, I wrote the notes," Henry confessed. "But I didn't take your stupid raccoon."

Amber stepped back, dumbfounded. "You—you don't have R.C.? But why did you write those notes?"

He grinned sheepishly. "I thought it was funny, the way you believed somebody kidnapped your raccoon. So I decided to make it look like somebody really *did* kidnap R.C. For fun."

"You sent the notes for fun? As a joke?"

He laughed. "I hid in the bushes the first time I sent the note. You should have seen your face!"

Amber flew at him again, her fingers curved into claws. "Wait till you see *your* face when I get done with it!"

This time Mindy and David pulled her away.

"No fighting," David ordered.

Amber turned on him. "You let your friend send me kidnap notes! Henry, how could you be so mean? How could both of you be so terrible?" She was nearly crying.

For once, Henry had the grace to be ashamed. "I'm sorry," he said. "I thought it was funny at the time. I guess it wasn't."

But Amber couldn't accept his apology. This time Henry Hoffstedder had gone too far.

Crushed with disappointment, she walked away before anyone could see her tears.

She'd been so sure she had the raccoon-napper. Whenever Billie Bradley accused a suspect, he confessed his crime immediately. Billie was never wrong.

But worse than being wrong, Amber decided, was

feeling that R.C. was as far away as ever.

"Mom called," Justin told Amber when she walked into the house. "She's got another date with Phillip tonight."

Amber's heart sank. She really needed her mother home tonight. Only her mother would understand how bad she felt learning the raccoon-napper was still at large.

"Is she coming home first?" Amber asked.

Justin shook his head. "She's leaving from the shop. She won't be home for dinner, but she left us money for pizza."

Amber's flagging spirits rallied a bit. She loved having pizza delivered. It was exciting when the pizza man came to the door and handed her the warm cardboard box. Maybe Justin would let her pay him, too.

"Are you going anywhere?" Justin asked her.

"I guess I'll go to Mindy's. Why?"

"Chris invited me over to play his new video game. But if you were staying home, I'd have to stay home." Justin took his job as baby sitter seriously.

"Well, you don't have to. I'm leaving for Mindy's now. I'll probably eat lunch over there, too," Amber said, heading back out the door.

Mrs. Alexander answered the door. "Mindy's in her room. Go on in."

Amber met Karen in the hallway. Mindy's sister looked startled when she saw Amber.

"Mindy!" she yelled at the top of her lungs. "Amber's here!"

"Good grief, Karen." Amber clamped her hands over her ears. "You don't have to scream like that."

She knocked on Mindy's bedroom door. "Open up," she called.

"Wait a sec," called Mindy's voice.

Amber tried the knob. It was locked. Mindy never locked her bedroom door. What was going on?

"Mindy, open up."

Mysterious thumping and bumping sounds came from within. "Just a minute!" Mindy yelled.

Finally she unlocked the door. Her face was pink, as if she'd been moving furniture.

"How come you locked the door? What are you doing?"

"Nothing," Mindy replied evasively.

"I thought we weren't going to have any more secrets," Amber accused.

"This isn't a secret. I was just—getting dressed. I didn't want anybody barging in. You don't have a little sister, Amber, so you don't know what it's like."

Mindy's sister didn't seem like the nosy type to Amber. Karen played by herself, when she wasn't at Delight's pool with them. She certainly kept to herself at the library program.

Amber was still too disappointed by this morning to argue. "Can you come out and play?"

Mindy shook her head. "Mom wants me to watch Sarah while she cleans the basement."

"Mom isn't going to clean the basement," Karen blabbed.

Amber caught Mindy's warning look. It was clear Mindy was hiding something from Amber. She obviously didn't want to play.

"Okay," Amber said huffily. "I can take a hint. If anybody wants me, I'll be at Delight's. My *new* best-best friend!"

She stalked out of Mindy's house, hoping Mindy would call her back and say she was sorry. But there was only silence behind her.

She couldn't go home. Justin wasn't there. She had no choice but to continue up the street to Delight's house.

Delight met her with a huge grin.

"Guess what?" she exclaimed.

"Your pool is filled with Kool-Aid?"

"No!" Delight laughed. "My mom said we don't have to move after all. We're staying here! Isn't that great news?"

"That *is* great news!" Now that Mindy was no longer her best-best friend, Amber was doubly glad that Delight wasn't moving.

"We'll all be in fourth grade together next year," Delight said.

Amber had forgotten about fourth grade. She had forgotten about the exciting summer she had planned to have, so she would have something to write about in her fourth grade essay. So far her summer had been one problem after another.

But at least *one* problem was solved. Delight was not moving away.

Mrs. Figley fixed them an extra-special lunch to celebrate. Then they swam the rest of the afternoon. When the sun sank low in the sky, Amber realized it was time to go home.

She called Justin first, so he wouldn't be worried. Before she left, Delight handed her a plastic shopping bag.

"What is this?" Amber asked.

"Look inside."

Amber peered into the bag and saw Row-bear, Delight's stuffed dog that had come all the way from Paris, France.

"Remember I said we could share Row-bear?" Delight told Amber. "You can borrow him."

"Are you sure?" Amber knew how tough it was to get along without a favorite stuffed animal.

"Positive. Keep him as long as you like."

At home, Amber took Row-bear out of the shopping bag and set him on her bed. Row-bear was almost as special as R.C. Maybe he would be an okay temporary replacement.

Justin phoned in their pizza order and let Amber watch for the pizza man.

Hot pizza delivered to their door tasted a lot better than pizza in a restaurant. Amber ate three slices.

"The best part," Justin said as he folded the empty carton, "is no dishes."

Amber went to bed early that night. She wanted to see if she could sleep, now that she had Row-bear.

She slipped between the sheets, propping Row-bear on the pillow next to her. After a few minutes, she reached over and picked up the stuffed dog. She held him in her arms, the way she used to hold R.C.

Delight's dog was soft and huggable, but he didn't feel like R.C. He didn't have one smooshed ear like R.C. either.

With a sigh, Amber put the stuffed dog on the floor. Row-bear was nice, but he couldn't fill the hole in her heart.

Only R.C. could do that.

Chapter
ELEVEN

Amber listlessly stirred her bowl of cereal. She hadn't slept well, not even with a borrowed dog all the way from Paris, France.

Her mother looked at her with concern. "Amber, are you okay?" She laid her hand on Amber's forehead. "You don't have a temperature. What is it then? Is it because I went out with Phillip again last night?"

"I don't mind if you go out," Amber replied. But she did mind. Since R.C. had disappeared, everything bothered her.

"Tell you what," her mother bargained. "If you cheer up, I'll take you and Mindy and Delight to the movies this evening. You pick the movie. How's that?"

"Not Mindy," Amber said emphatically.

"What do you mean, not Mindy? You don't want to ask Mindy?"

Amber pushed her half-eaten cereal away. "She

won't go. She doesn't want to be friends with me."

"I don't believe that!" her mother said. "Why, you and Mindy have been best friends for years."

"Not anymore."

Her mother took Amber's cereal bowl to the sink to rinse. "You and Mindy have just had a little tiff. It will blow over. These things always do. If you like, I'll call Mindy's mother about the movie this evening."

"You're just wasting your breath," Amber said.

Her mother didn't understand that she and Mindy hadn't had a little tiff. In Amber's mind, the problem between them was huge, bigger than the biggest boulder. Amber didn't see how she could budge it.

Even though it was early, Amber walked to Delight's house to return Row-bear.

"Thanks a lot," she told Delight. "It was nice of you to let me borrow him."

"But he's not the same as R.C., is he?" Delight said. "Mindy and I have soccer practice this morning. Want to come watch?" Delight didn't know about their latest fight.

Amber shook her head. "I have my library program. Maybe I can come swim after lunch."

"I have to go out this afternoon," Delight said.

"Well, we'll see each other this evening. My mom is going to ask your mom if you can go to the movies."

"Sounds great," Delight said. "See you later."

At the library, Miss Marsh handed Amber a book. "Have you read this one?"

Amber looked at the title, *The Dancing Ghost*. It

was number thirteen in the Billie Bradley series. "No, I haven't read it. Thanks, Miss Marsh."

"Good. Will you amuse the kids at the table while I try to keep Kyle and Aaron from killing each other?"

Amber went over to the table. The little kids were sharing a picture book. Karen saw Amber and checked under her seat where she kept her big paper bag. A lot of the children brought a snack to eat during break time.

"Hi, Karen," she said.

"Hello. I'm going swimming today."

"You are? That's nice." She paused. "How's Mindy?"

Karen shrugged. "Okay, I guess. Are you still mad at her?"

This time Amber shrugged. "I didn't start it. She did."

Karen bit her lip. She seemed about to tell Amber something when Miss Marsh began the program.

At home later, Amber opened her new Billie Bradley book. This one wasn't as good as the others. Maybe she was getting tired of Billie Bradley mysteries. The next time she went to the library, she'd get something different.

When someone knocked on the front door, she let Justin answer it. She heard the brief rise and fall of voices, then silence. It was probably somebody trying to sell magazines.

"Hi," said a familiar voice.

Surprised, Amber looked up and saw Mindy standing in her doorway. She carried a large gift bag splashed with rainbows.

"Can I come in?" Mindy asked.

"Sure." Amber put her book down.

Mindy handed her the gift bag. "I brought you this."

Amber took the bag, giving Mindy a curious look. First Mindy was here on a surprise visit. Then she was giving her a present. Did this mean she wanted to make up?

"Go ahead, open it," Mindy urged. She sounded nervous.

Amber peeked in the bag. With a gasp, she stared at Mindy. "R.C.! You brought him back!"

"Not exactly," Mindy explained. "Take him out and you'll see."

Amber lifted the stuffed animal from the sack. As she did, she knew it wasn't R.C. Her heart dropped to her toes.

The stuffed animal was supposed to be a raccoon. The plush fur was striped like a raccoon's, and there was a black mask across its eyes like a raccoon's. But the body was shaped more like a gorilla's. It was lumpy, and the arms and legs were sewn on with large, clumsy stitches.

Amber had never seen an uglier stuffed animal. Where on earth had Mindy gotten it?

"I made it myself," Mindy said proudly. "Mom helped me pick out a pattern at the sewing store. I bought the furry cloth with my allowance."

"You made this?"

Mindy nodded. "All by myself. Nobody helped me. Well, Mom held its head on while I sewed it to the body, but that's all."

Amber stroked the crooked ears. "Is this what you were doing those times I came over and you kept shutting the door?"

"I wanted it to be a surprise," Mindy said. "You've been so down in the dumps without R.C. So I made you a new one. I was going to give it to you for your birthday, but I couldn't wait. Maybe you can call him R.C. II."

Amber touched the yellow ribbon around the raccoon's neck. She didn't know what to say.

Mindy drew in a shaky breath. "Do you like him?"

"I love him," Amber said, and meant it. She'd never received a more wonderful present.

She remembered that day two years ago when her father gave her a brand-new R.C. with smooth, shiny fur and two perky ears. Something had happened when her father put the stuffed raccoon in her arms. Amber had fallen in love. And even though her father was leaving, she realized she had something to hold on to during the bad times.

Now something happened when Mindy gave her the homemade raccoon. She realized she didn't need R.C. anymore. Not the way she used to need him.

People were more important than a stuffed animal. She had a terrific best-best friend, a great second-best friend, and a family who loved her. Hadn't they all showed they cared about her?

Maybe this was what her teacher had meant when she said Amber had learned many things in third grade besides spelling and fractions.

Amber put Mindy's raccoon on her bed, in the place of honor.

"R.C. II is a good name," she said. "That's what I'll call him. And he'll stay on my bed, just like R.C. used to."

Justin poked his head around the door. "Lunchtime."

"Can you stay?" Amber asked Mindy.

Mindy called her mother and got permission. They took their sandwiches outside on the patio. Amber was telling Mindy about the movie they were going to see later when the phone rang.

It was Mrs. Alexander. She wanted to talk to Mindy.

When Mindy hung up, her freckled face was pale.

"Karen's missing," she said. "Mom said she was in the front yard playing and now she's not."

"Maybe she's in the house."

Mindy shook her head. "Mom looked. She's not anywhere."

A chill trickled down Amber's spine. It was like the day R.C. had mysteriously disappeared from the patio!

Mrs. Alexander hurried into the yard, carrying Sarah. "I've been up and down the street," she said frantically. "I can't find Karen anywhere!"

Justin leaped to his feet. "I'll round up Chris.

We'll cover the neighborhood. Don't worry, Mrs. Alexander. We'll find her."

Mrs. Alexander sank down onto the swing. "I can't believe this is happening. I was watching Karen through the window, and then Mindy called to ask if she could stay over here for lunch. When I looked, Karen was gone."

Just like R.C., Amber thought. No, not like R.C. Karen wasn't a stuffed animal. She was Mindy's sister. And they had to find her.

Amber tried to remember Billie Bradley's technique for organizing a search.

"If Karen could go anyplace she wanted," Amber asked Mindy, "where would that be?"

"Disney World," was Mindy's immediate response.

"No, I mean around here."

"Well, she likes going to the store—"

Suddenly Amber realized where Karen had gone. But suppose she was wrong? No, she wasn't wrong. Her detective instincts told her she was right this time.

"I know where she is!"

Amber leaped off the patio. The others followed, but Amber was the fastest.

Like a wild horse, she galloped up Carriage Street. Her hair streamed behind her like a mane as she charged across the bridge over Little Rocky Run and up the hill to Delight's house. She wasn't a good runner in soccer, but she could run like the wind when she had to.

She flew across the Wakefields' front yard, then skidded to a stop at the fence.

The gate. She had forgotten about the gate. Of course it would be locked. And Karen was too small to climb over that high board fence.

Sure enough, Karen was standing on tiptoe at the gate, struggling to open it. When she heard footsteps behind her, she whirled. She held something tightly in her arms.

Amber stared at the object.

It was a stuffed raccoon with one lopsided ear and the fur lovingly rubbed off on its face.

R.C.

The others hurried up.

"Karen!" cried Mrs. Alexander. "You're okay!" Handing Sarah to Mindy, she scooped up Karen and hugged her.

"Good guess," Mindy said to Amber. "I should have thought of here. Karen's always bugging me to take her to Delight's pool."

"Sorry I didn't have time to tell you," Amber said, catching her breath. "I just had this hunch."

"I'm glad you acted impulsively," said Mrs. Alexander. "When I think of what could have happened—"

Justin tested the lock on the gate. "It's still locked. She couldn't have gotten in."

"But you gave us a good scare. Don't ever wander off again!" Mrs. Alexander scolded Karen. "You know you're not allowed to leave the yard by yourself."

No one seemed to notice the stuffed animal Karen

clutched. They were all happy to have found her. Amber was happy, too, but she couldn't stand it any longer.

"She's got R.C.!" she blurted.

Mrs. Alexander plucked the stuffed animal out of Karen's grasp. "Why, this *is* R.C. Karen, what are you doing with Amber's stuffed animal?"

Now Karen began to cry. Mrs. Alexander set her down and wiped her nose with a tissue.

"Karen," Amber said gently. "It's okay. You're not in trouble. I just want to know how you got R.C."

Karen snuffled. "I took him off your swing."

So she was the one who had stolen R.C.! The mystery was finally solved.

"Why did you take Amber's toy?" Mrs. Alexander asked.

"Because I wanted it," Karen said simply. "R.C. is neat. He even goes to school. I don't have anything like R.C."

Mrs. Alexander spoke apologetically to Amber. "I had no idea she had taken your stuffed animal. She must have hidden it well."

"I did," Karen said.

"I never suspected Karen had him either. Where did you hide him?" Mindy asked her sister.

"Lots of places. My room. Behind the furnace. I even took him to the library in a bag," Karen answered with pride.

"I thought that was your snack!" Amber couldn't believe she'd been looking high and low for R.C. and he'd been under her nose the whole time.

"That wasn't nice," Mrs. Alexander said to Karen. "You took something that didn't belong to you. You know you're not supposed to do that, Karen. What do you say?"

Karen began to sob again. She surrendered R.C. to Amber. "Here, Amber. I'm sorry I took him."

Amber examined R.C. He didn't look any worse for being raccoon-napped most of the summer. His smooshed ear was a bit more lopsided. And more fur was worn off on one side of his face. But other than that, he seemed fine.

"It's okay," she said. "Really. I'm not mad at you."

Karen smiled through her tears. "I like R.C. He's neat."

"Well, maybe you can borrow him sometime," Amber offered. "Maybe he can spend the night with you. *If* you promise not to leave the yard again. Okay?"

"Okay," Karen promised.

They all walked back down the street. Amber and Mindy trailed behind the others.

Amber held R.C. under her arm. It felt good having him back. Now she would have two raccoons on her pillow. She would never have trouble getting to sleep again. All the things that had been bothering her were fading away.

"I guess this is the end of the Carriage Street Crime-Busters," Mindy said. "Now that the case is solved."

Amber thought how her new Billie Bradley book wasn't all that interesting. She liked being a detective, but she wanted to do other things as well.

"We can still have the detective agency," she said. "But let's do other stuff, too."

"Can I be head detective sometime?" Mindy asked. "Delight, too?"

"Sure." Amber didn't need to be like Billie Bradley anymore. It occurred to her that her heroine didn't have much fun.

They paused on the bridge and gazed over the rail.

"Mom says summer is half over," Mindy commented. "I can't believe you and me and Delight will be fourth-graders soon."

"Me neither," Amber said. "In fourth grade we'll go to Williamsburg on the class trip—"

"And take music and work on the school newspaper—"

"And write our vacation essays," Amber said.

Mindy kicked a stone off the bridge into the water below. "I don't have any idea what I'll write about."

Amber did. Instead of writing about *her* summer vacation, she would write about R.C.'s adventures. What an exciting summer he'd had!

Suddenly she felt the urge to run. She ran joyfully down Carriage Street.

Summer wasn't over yet. And Amber Gillian Cantrell still had a lot of wild-horse days ahead of her.